HOW TO GET SUSPENDED and INFLUENCE PEOPLE

PEOPLE

A NOVEL BY
ADAM SELZER

delacorte press

Published by Delacorte Press
an imprint of Random House Children's Books
a division of Random House, Inc.
New York

www.randomhouse.com/teens

Educators and librarians, for a variety of teaching tools,
visit us at www.randomhouse.com/teachers

Library of Congress Cataloging-in-Publication Data
Selzer, Adam.
How to get suspended and influence people / by Adam Selzer.
p. cm.
Summary: Gifted eighth-grader Leon Harris becomes an instant
celebrity when the film he makes for a class project sends him to
in-school suspension.
ISBN: 978-0-385-73369-4 (trade ed.)
ISBN: 978-0-385-90384-4 (lib. ed.)
[1. Motion pictures—Production and direction—Fiction. 2. Gifted
children—Fiction. 3. Middle schools—Fiction. 4. Schools—Fiction.]
I. Title.
CURR PZ7.S4652How 2007 2006
[Fic]—dc22
2006020438

The text of this book is set in 12-point Goudy.

Printed in the United States of America

10 9 8 7 6 5 4 3 2 1

First Edition

To my fellow veterans of Urbandale Middle School.
I came, I sat, I departed.

Acknowledgments

First of all, thanks to my family, who never even suggested that I go to accounting school. Also thanks to Nadia, my fantastic agent. Finally, thanks to Sean, Merideth, Cindy, Abbie, David, Seth, Tanner, Brian, Mike, et al., from my middle school years. I never would have survived without you guys.

1

It's a good thing my father is an accountant, because he really sucks at being an inventor. It's not that he hasn't given 110 percent or any of that crap; it's just that he never quite got the fundamentals right. For one thing, inventions are supposed to work. Furthermore, they're supposed to be things that don't already exist. He really can't get his mind around that.

"Do you know what the world needs?" he asked one night. "A machine that will automatically pour water into a cat's dish."

I tried to explain that such a machine already existed, but he didn't listen. Even when I showed him the various models that were available at our local pet store, he said that to simply buy something you could invent yourself, using good old American ingenuity, is practically unpatriotic. I tried to explain that buying products is what capitalism is all about, and that it's therefore perfectly patriotic, which anyone who ever took a sixth-grade civics class should have known to begin with, but he didn't listen to that, either. Instead, he worked for three months, and flooded the basement twice, building a machine that I suppose might have worked but that might also have been a dud. There was no way to tell. The cat wouldn't go near the thing.

Dad's inventions aren't the only dangerous things I have to put up with; the meals at my house are just as deadly, and often frankly embarrassing. It isn't that my mother's a bad cook or anything; hell, as far as I know, she could be the best cook in town. But she and my dad are what they call "food disaster hobbyists." It's like being the sort of person who watches bad movies on purpose just to make fun of them, only with food.

My parents' idea of a good time is going down to the thrift store and buying old cookbooks from the fifties and sixties, ones with titles like *The Wonders of Lard* and *You and Your Artichokes*. I don't know if you've ever seen one of those, but some of the pictures and recipes in them look absolutely wretched. Every few weekends, my parents buy up a stack of them and spend hours laughing at some of the worst recipes, and then, for reasons I have never been able to fathom, once or twice a week they cook them and serve them for dinner. It's one of their many poor, misguided attempts at "quality family time." Dad's inventions can get a bit embarrassing or dangerous, but cooking terrible recipes on purpose and expecting your kid to eat them simply isn't very nice. Mom and Dad insist that the recipes aren't really bad, just different, and even point out that now and then one turns out to be pretty good, but the odds on that are really pretty dismal. Even orphans in the old days got to eat good old reliable gruel. Nobody tried to make the gruel into an even nastier casserole.

On the night after my first day of eighth grade, I really didn't want to go through with the usual family dinner, since I knew that they'd just bought up another batch of cookbooks they probably couldn't wait to try.

"So, Leon," said my father as we sat down, "how was the first day of school?"

"Fine," I mumbled as my mother heaped a much larger pile of some mysterious form of casserole than I would have liked onto my plate. The casserole clashed badly with the dinnerware, which was from what I guess you'd call the 1950s Vomitesque school of household design, like the ugly, paste-colored trays with swirling designs that we used to have at the cafeteria in elementary school. Even the harvest gold and avocado green of the 1970s haven't been out of style long enough for my mother to get on the bandwagon.

"That's it?" my father asked. "Just fine?"

"He's not telling us something," said my mother, as if I wasn't present. "What aren't you telling us, Leon?"

I shoveled a large spoonful of the casserole into my mouth and chewed it long and hard. This was not a particularly pleasant thing to do, but it was worth it to stall having to talk.

"Well," I finally said, "when we were all introducing ourselves in math class, they made us all say our middle names." This, of course, is a classic first-day-of-school time waster for teachers who aren't very creative.

"What's wrong with that?" my father asked.

"I told them my middle name was Harold," I said.

They put down their silverware and stared at me for a second, as though they wanted an explanation. "Well?" I asked. "What was I supposed to do? I couldn't very well tell them that my middle name is Noside! That could wreck my reputation clear into high school!"

Keeping people from finding out what my middle name is has been a battle as long as I've been in school. When I die, I'm going to come back as a ghost to make sure it isn't on my tombstone.

"That name," said my father angrily as he slammed down his glass of water, causing a few drops to splash onto the table, "is more than just a name, it's a responsibility."

In case I haven't properly established this fact, my father is crazy. I'm convinced that no sane person would name his child Leon in this day and age, and I'm further convinced that anyone who would give his child the middle name Noside is probably a danger to himself and others. I suppose I should count myself lucky that he didn't name me Eureka, which my uncle once told me Dad had wanted to do. I'd never get through middle school alive with a name that sounds like "you reek-a."

I scooped up more of the casserole and popped it into my mouth to keep myself from groaning. I do a lot of groaning around the house, and I knew that my father was about to start in on the lecture I always get when I bring up the middle name. This particular lecture had been the cause of countless groans over the years.

"Noside," he began solemnly, "is Edison spelled backwards. You were given that name as an insult to the late

4

Thomas Edison, who was a jerk who took credit for other people's work. Your middle name carries on our responsibility as decent people to expose him as a fraud."

My father is practically obsessed with hating Thomas Edison. Personally, I'm convinced that my father's real problem with Thomas Edison is that he's jealous that Edison invented a lot of good stuff before he had the chance. And I'm further convinced that Thomas Edison himself doesn't feel the least bit insulted by my middle name, what with being dead and all.

But the lecture made perfect sense to both of my parents, who stared up at the ceiling for the next few minutes, as though they were looking toward God, or, more likely, the spirit of Thomas Edison, to ask what was wrong with me. *Why oh why,* they were probably thinking, *hasn't our only begotten son grown into an Edison-hating inventor who makes intentionally bad meals? He's in eighth grade now, and he'll be in high school next year—can we possibly turn him into a complete loser in time for him to get into accounting school?* They stared at the ceiling like this a lot; I was in second grade before I found out that Thomas Edison was just a regular guy. Before then, I'd thought he was some sort of deity or something and worried that if anyone found out that my dad hated him, we'd get kicked out of church.

When Mom and Dad finally started speaking, they changed the topic altogether to the quality of the dinner, which, from what I could tell, involved raisins, mayonnaise, and something that might have been tuna but somehow tasted like ketchup.

"This is absolutely bizarre," said my father, grinning from ear to ear. "The flavors just . . . clash!"

"Can you believe they actually published this recipe, Leon?" asked my mother, who was clearly delighted that they had. I resisted her sly trick to get me into the spirit of the whole meal. I had my pride.

"I can just imagine the guy writing it," said my dad. He began to speak in a bad French accent. "Aha! What zis mayonnaise needs is . . . more raisins!"

"How shockingly bold!" said my mother, in her own bad French accent.

This is pretty much the way every food disaster dinner plays out. I'm expected to participate, because if I don't, it's not "quality family time," but I rarely say a word, and they aren't very good at coming up with funny things to say about the food themselves. It seems to me that if you're going to make your kid watch you make a complete dork of yourself, you could at least have the courtesy to come up with better jokes.

Despite the rough start, I was glad to be back in school, if only to see my friends again. I'd finally been allowed to take my bike across Venture Street over the summer, which was like busting out of jail, and which meant that I had been able to see more of my friends than I had the last several summers. But we hadn't all been together in a while.

Of course, the first week of school wasn't that exciting; they never really have you doing much in class those first few days, and there wasn't much in the way of hijinks. We didn't even start our normal schedules until the second week, and in the classes we did have, all was quiet. Everyone was actually well behaved. It seemed like the year before, when things had gotten out of control in class just about every day, had never even happened. But I knew things would pick up soon. My faith in my fellow students was strong.

On Saturday morning, my father asked if I'd like to go

to the flea market with him, and, having forgotten all about our latest fight about my middle name, I said I'd love to. I'd found out some time before that you could buy old stereo speakers, often very large ones, for a couple of bucks at a lot of flea markets, and had figured that if I got enough of them, and enough connectors and splitters to hook them all up to my stereo, I could cover a whole wall of my bedroom with speakers. My very own wall of sound! As of that Saturday, I had covered about half the wall but hadn't had the nerve to try them out yet.

As we drove along in the van, my father started to talk about his latest invention.

"I'm going to the flea market for parts," he said, as if I couldn't have guessed. "I've decided to invent a single switch that will turn off all the electricity in the house at once."

"They have those," I told him. "They're called circuit boxes. We keep ours in the garage."

"Bah," he said, waving a hand that he should probably have kept on the steering wheel. "That's a whole bunch of complicated switches. The other day I was trying to shut off the power so I could install a new light in the living room without getting an electric shock, and I said to myself, 'There has to be a better way.' That's where I come in!"

I would have said that I'd need to be careful to save my work on the computer regularly because the power would probably be shutting off randomly while he was doing tests, but I was convinced that even if he blew up the entire house in the process of building this invention, the electricity would still be running in the rubble. Of course, if I told him that, he would just take it as a vote of confidence that he could make something capable of blowing up the house. It was a strict rule of mine never to do or say anything that could be construed as encouragement for my dad's inventions. I figured that the more I encouraged him, the sooner he'd set the garage on fire. He'd come pretty close on several occasions.

When we got to the flea market, we went off in separate directions. Before hitting the speakers, I flipped through the boxes of tapes for a bit and found a couple of old Black Sabbath albums. Liking heavy metal had saved me on several occasions; middle schoolers on the whole did not look kindly on kids who, like me, didn't bother with sports, but since I liked heavy metal, I was sort of given a pass. It made me just cool enough to avoid getting beaten up.

After an hour or so, I met up with Dad at the door, with two Black Sabbath tapes, two very large speakers, and a bunch of speaker wire in hand. He was carrying a bunch of cables, some switches, a handful of gears that looked broken, and a test tube. I didn't ask what he was planning to do with the test tube. Frankly, I didn't want to know.

"Leon," he said as we pulled out of the parking lot, "would you like to help me on this project?"

"No thanks," I said as politely as I could. "I like keeping the electricity in the house *on*."

"But you'd be aiding in the creating of an invention that will benefit mankind, possibly for centuries to come!" he said in his best patriotic inventor voice. "Won't that look great on a college application?"

"Dad," I said, "if you ever want the electricity turned off, just tell me, and I'll happily do it for you. I have other things to do today."

"Leon," he said, sounding annoyed, "I just want to expand your horizons. Obviously you're interested in electronics. You're always buying gear to hook up those speakers."

I didn't tell him that I hadn't actually hooked them up yet.

"And more to the point," he said, "we need to spend more quality time together."

"Dad," I said, "I won't be a party to helping you spend hours tinkering around building something that already exists and is rarely of any use. It's not as though you'll ever get it to work right."

I regretted saying that immediately. For one thing, it wasn't very nice. Furthermore, I was under strict orders from my mother never to point out my dad's inability to invent things that worked.

Dad didn't respond for a long time. But as we were getting close to home, he said, "Leon, I know that I've had a lot of setbacks, but if inventors just gave up because of setbacks, nothing would ever get invented. You should always keep trying; it's the American way. I'm going to make this work, Leon. And one day, I'll invent something that will set my whole field on fire!"

Dad's goal as an inventor is to one day create something that will revolutionize the world of accounting, but so far, he's failed to come up with right idea. I think that once the pocket calculator came along, accountants had gone about as far as they could go. Every time he talks about revolutionizing the accountant, I picture one of those paintings of the

French Revolution from my history book, only instead of the working class leading people to have their heads chopped off, it was accountants. Nerdy ones.

You know how sometimes silence sounds like a lecture? This was one of those times. I really wished there was some way I could subtly give him some encouragement, something to make him feel better. I could tell by the fact that he wasn't saying much that I'd really hurt his feelings; if I hadn't, he would have been talking my ear off about his plans for the latest invention. I didn't want to break my personal rule against encouragement, but, well, he's my dad. I felt bad about saying mean things like that to him. After all, it's not nice to be mean to crazy people.

When we got out of the car, he went straight to the garage to start working, and I went up to my room. I had decided that I wanted to try hooking up all my speakers, just to hear how things sounded. And anyway, staying busy kept me from feeling guilty.

So I hung the new speakers on the wall with the others I'd collected, then spent the better part of two hours hooking them all up to various connectors, ports, and splitters and hooking the whole thing into the stereo. By the time I was finished, my room was a mess of wires. I'd have to think of a good way to cover them up sooner or later. I considered getting a rug with some band's logo on it.

I'd put a lot of thought into what song I should play first when testing the wall of sound, and after narrowing it down to five choices and discussing them with my friends, I'd decided on "Back in Black," by AC/DC. I was originally going to go with "Stairway to Heaven," which seemed like an obvious choice, but "Stairway" starts off pretty slow. "Back in Black" cuts right into the loud electric guitar riff at the very beginning.

I had a CD consisting of only that song in my dresser, which I'd made a long time before just for this occasion. I dug it out, stuck it in the stereo, and hit Play.

Exactly one unbelievably loud guitar chord came out of all of the speakers on the wall. I swear the house shook a bit, and I imagine that all the birds in the trees probably flew away in one big flock, like they do when a gun goes off in the movies but the director doesn't want to show anybody getting shot. But after that one chord, there was a big pop and a bunch of sparks. Most of the sparks were little ones around the speakers, but there was a big one by the electrical outlet where the stereo was plugged in. Then the music stopped, and the lights went out, and all the appliances in the room went dead. Not just the stereo, but the clock radio, the lamp, and the beat-up TV I had that only worked for video games. Apparently I'd blown a fuse or two. All the electricity in the house appeared to be out.

Five seconds later, through the buzzing in my ears, I heard the voice of my father downstairs.

"Eureka!" he shouted.

Weekends in the summer are always lame. Weekdays settle into a nice routine in which all the regular reruns are on and my parents aren't home, but everything gets messed up on the weekends. The best part about being back in school was that my weekends went back to normal. Well, normal for a kid in a house full of escaped mental patients, anyway.

My father got back to normal (for him) right away, too. At first he was really disappointed when he found out that the electricity going off had been my doing, not his, but after a while, he decided that he was proud of me.

"My son," he said, in his best fatherly voice, "some parents might be furious that their child blew a fuse with heavy metal, but I'm not one of those. I'm proud of you. You were trying to invent something, in a way. Even if it didn't work, it's a very noble endeavor to try to invent something."

I would have been happier if he'd just been furious. I'm pretty sure he was just relieved that I hadn't blown up most of the house. In any case, I put the wall of sound project on the back burner for a while.

The weekend passed as quickly as most weekends do, and on Monday morning it was time for school to start back up, and Monday came and went, but it was Tuesday that I was looking forward to. The midweek mornings were different.

Starting the second week, on Tuesday, Wednesday, and Thursday mornings, instead of homeroom, all of the sixth and seventh graders went to "advisory," where they sat around and talked about heavy issues like drugs, drinking, and teen pregnancy. I had been convinced, back when I started sixth grade, that advisory would be boring, and had been further convinced that there wouldn't be anything covered in class that we hadn't seen a hundred times on after-school specials.

But there had always been rumors that middle school sex ed, which was part of advisory, involved actual photographs, so I couldn't help looking forward to it a little bit. Not that I didn't know what naked people looked like or anything—I had the Internet, after all—but that wasn't quite the same as getting to see them in class. But it turned out that I had been right all along; there was nothing in the class we hadn't all heard a thousand times before, and all of the pictures in sex ed were lame diagrams and line drawings.

While I understood that they still taught the same class under the name "health" at the high school, for some reason they gave us a break in eighth grade, and instead of advisory, we'd be going to "activity period." The first week of school, we'd each signed up for an activity. Most people had signed up for team sports or Ping-Pong, and a couple of the truly sick had signed up for "good grooming."

I'd gotten my homeroom teacher's permission to sign up for the advanced studies activity, which was a fancy way of saying "the smart class." This really should have seemed un-cool, but it wasn't, because I knew it would just be all the kids from the gifted pool who met with an old bat named Mrs. Smollet once a week. It was kind of fun; we sat in the couches that had been set up, and while we were supposed to be doing brain teasers or crossword puzzles or something like that, we made it our business to try to bug the crap out of Mrs. Smollet, who was kind of a goody-goody religious type and was a little bit afraid of us. I'm not sure where they came up with a name like "gifted pool." It's the kind of name only a teacher at the end of his or her rope could have devised.

Now, on TV or in the movies, whenever the main char-acter is a boy genius or something, the smart classes are made up of dorks who tuck their shirts into their underwear, do math in their heads, and might actually sign up for the good grooming activity. In reality, our advanced classes and gifted pools were always made up of a bunch of miscreant kids who just happened to read books from the adult section of the library. Many of us even read newspapers. That was all. The real dorks weren't smart enough to get in.

My activity group was meeting in the media immersion room, which is what they called the room that used to be called the library. During the previous couple of years, they'd added a whole bunch of new computers and other high-tech stuff and changed the name, but it was basically the same place.

I saw right away that the advanced studies activity was the usual band of troublemakers, all sitting in chairs that had been arranged in a circle. There was James Cole, who spoke fluent French and was the first kid in school to smoke pot. Next to him was Dustin Eddlebeck, who had graduated from writing naughty limericks on the bathroom walls to writing naughty sonnets, which were much longer. Then there was Edie Scaduto, the school communist, sitting next to Brian Carlson, her boyfriend, who was really into fire, and a handful of other kids I didn't know quite as well. If it wasn't for the fact that we were gifted-pool kids, I'm sure the school would have gone to great lengths to keep us far away from each other at all times. I guess you could say we had a pretty good scam going.

My friend Anna was already there, too. She had cut her blond hair to her shoulders—it used to be down to her butt—but I decided not to mention it. She hated it when people rambled on about her long hair.

"Hey, Anna," I said, sitting down next to her, and enough chairs away from Brian Carlson that I didn't have to worry about getting my shoelaces set on fire. "How was your summer?"

"Pleasurable," she said.

Anna is the one person in school who has weirder parents than mine. They were in college for about twenty years each and probably know just about everything in the world.

Her dad is a professor of something or other in the city, and her mother occasionally flies to Europe to see if some painting that turned up at a flea market in Amsterdam is actually a Cézanne or just a fake—I suppose you could say she's like an art detective. The one time I've been in Anna's house, when I went to deliver homework to her when she was sick, there were framed prints of weird paintings all over the walls and incense burning on the kitchen table, and she called her parents by their first names. And her father had a bookshelf covering one entire wall, filled with books about the eighteenth century. There were a whole bunch of musical instruments in the living room, and apparently Anna's parents play all of them and have made Anna take cello lessons since she was three.

And here's the weird thing: Anna actually likes them. She's always showing off cool yoga poses or coming up to me to say things like, "Did you know that most eighteenth-century French literature was originally published outside of France?" I guess I would like my parents if they were more like that. Anna's mom and dad are sort of sophisticated and cool, instead of just plain weird and potentially dangerous. You can bet that they won't be expecting her to go to accounting school when she finishes high school.

It goes without saying, of course, that Anna is less than popular. Outside of the advanced classes, spouting off facts about the eighteenth century and playing the cello aren't the best ways to get ahead in middle school. But I like her. She's cool and really very cute. Naturally, I wouldn't have said that out loud, least of all to her, for anything. The thought of going on a date with my dad giving us a ride was more than enough to keep my mouth shut.

My activity period teacher turned out to be Mr. Streich, one of the science teachers, who my father knows fairly well; they occasionally go shopping for parts together. I took this to be a bad sign. His named is pronounced like "strike." As in strike three. He has a mustache on purpose. Mustaches can make certain guys look pretty smooth, but most of them just look like a dorky sort of plumber. Even my father had refrained from growing a mustache. I suppose it was better than having Mrs. Smollet as the teacher, though.

"Good morning, students," said Mr. Streich. "You'll notice that I didn't call you boys and girls. You're in eighth grade now." I looked around the room but didn't see anyone looking any older than they had the year before. No one had grown a goatee over summer vacation. "Now," he continued, "this class may not actually be called advisory, but we'll still be talking about a lot of the stuff you've talked about for the last two years." Everyone groaned except Anna, who made more of a low, breathy moaning sound.

"We'll be talking about a lot of weighty issues," Mr. Streich continued, "but since this is the media immersion room, we're also going to spend a lot of our time working on multimedia projects as part of our advanced studies. I trust you've all seen plenty of health, safety, and sexual education videos before, right?"

We all nodded. I'd seen a lot of school movies, of course. Science movies tended to be the most boring; in seventh grade our teacher showed us one called *The Story of Osmosis*.

They tried to make it interesting by sticking a robot in there to tell kids about science, but they could've put in a hundred robots, all armed with laser guns, and it still wouldn't have held my interest for ten minutes, let alone an hour and a half. The really sad thing is that the robot sort of reminded me of my father.

But the sex-ed videos were the dumbest, even if they were a lot more entertaining than the science stuff. They'd started out with names like *How You Came to Be* and *Changes: Coming Soon to a Body Near You!* in fifth-grade science class. They were silly cartoons that tried to give us the bare-bones facts about sex and adolescence, even though we all already knew them by then.

In middle school, the films got more interesting, and we spent a lot of time outside of class making fun of them. We never remembered their real titles, so we made up ones that we thought were more appropriate to describe them, like *Johnny's Not a Baldy Anymore; Intrigue in the Locker Room; Looking Awkward, Feeling Awkward;* and *Billy's Got a Problem.* Every now and then you'd hear that the high school kids got to watch more more explicit films with names like *The Art of Reproduction* and *How Susie Got Sick in Florida.* That struck me as unlikely.

"Now," said Mr. Streich, "instead of just showing you a lot of those, over the course of the next month, each of you is going to make your own advisory video, using the equipment we have right here in the media room."

There was a bit of murmuring among the students.

"Now, we won't just be jumping right in with the filming. I know you all learned how to use the cameras and equipment last year in media immersion classes, so we're going to spend the first day or two just brainstorming about what kind of movies you'd like to make. Then you'll spend a while discussing your subject and doing research. These films will be shown to kids in grades six and seven at the end of the quarter, and we want to make sure you get all the facts right, whether you're making a movie about eating disorders, alcoholism, or smoking."

It sounded to me like the school was just trying to spare the expense of buying a bunch of new videos, but I had to admit that the project sounded like fun. When Mr. Streich passed around the list of possible subjects, I looked them over and was a bit surprised to see that sex ed was on the list. They were actually going to trust an eighth grader to make a sex-ed video? Were they drunk when they wrote out the list of topics? It was like being handed a live grenade and being invited to lob it at one of the teachers. Eating disorders struck me as a good topic, too, because you'd have a great excuse to do a puking scene, but I couldn't say no to the chance to make a sex-ed video that every student really wanted to see. I wrote my name next to "sex ed" on the list right away, before anyone else could get it. I was starting to get ideas before I'd even passed the sheet to Anna. And the wheels in my head began to turn.

No kid in any grade wanted to see some lame video with a bunch of line drawings of private parts. Everyone knows that, starting in fifth grade, every kid wants the sex-ed films to be as explicit as possible, and I was sure that if mine was bizarre enough to be considered "artsy," I could get away with putting just about anything in there. I could say, "It's not smut, it's art!" According to what I'd heard in social studies, I figured the Supreme Court would back me up.

And I wouldn't just be explicit, I'd be informative, about real stuff that kids actually wondered about, like how old they should be when they started worrying about not developing yet, how big things should be at a certain age. Stuff like that. We'd all seen movie after movie telling us we were normal, but hearing it from the disemodied voice of some weirdo over a goofy cartoon of a sperm cell in a top hat wasn't convincing anyone. Maybe if they heard it from a more artistic source, they'd believe it.

I didn't pay much attention to my classes for the rest of the morning because I was coming up with ideas for how I could make just such a video. First of all, I'd give it a French title. Or maybe an Italian one. As soon as you see a movie title in a foreign language, you know you're in for something artsy. Instead of boring narration, I'd have boring poetry that didn't make a whole lot of sense. I'd use nudes from famous paintings instead of diagrams. Realistic ones. With close-ups on the good parts.

I mulled the idea over until it was time for lunch, at which I sat with a bunch of people from my activity group, including Anna. I had made my own lunch; the school cooking wasn't much better than the average homemade food disaster, but I can make a pretty serviceable sandwich myself.

"How's it going?" I asked.

"Fine," she said, taking a sip of grape juice. She had brought her lunch, too.

"What topic did you pick for your video?" I had been so

wrapped up in my own film that I hadn't even had a chance to ask Anna about hers.

"Smoking," she said. "I'm thinking of doing one about how smoking really isn't all that bad for you."

"Isn't it?"

She shrugged. "I just figure that maybe it's time for a new approach. Those movies about how smoking wrecks your lungs aren't stopping anybody." This was true. It seemed like half of the kids I knew smoked at least every now and then, even though our teachers had been drilling how bad it was into our heads since kindergarten.

"I'm going to do a sex-ed movie," I said. "An artsy one."

"What do you mean?"

"I figure if I make one that's artsy, I can get away with showing more nudity."

She grinned. "You looking for models?"

I wondered if she was offering to do it, and started to feel woozy for a second, but I just said, "We can't do anything with actual nudity, remember?" Dustin Eddlebeck had asked right away, even though his movie was about seat belts, and Mr. Streich very quickly said absolutely not, even if the models were of legal age. No photographs of naked people, either. But he didn't say anything about paintings, and I knew enough not to ask.

"So what kind of artsy do you mean? Italian realist? German Expressionist? Avant-garde?"

"What exactly is avant-garde?" I asked. I'd heard the term a few times, but never with a definition attached. Anna's parents probably had a whole room full of avant-garde stuff, whatever it was.

"It's really weird art," she said. "The kind where people are painted blue and talk about truth and existence and then run around making noises like barnyard animals. Supposedly John Lennon once said 'avant-garde' is French for 'bullshit.' "

"I could probably make that work," I said. "I'm going to go for highbrow. Sophisticated, but still interesting. What's the brainiest movie your parents have?" I had never heard her talk about their movie collection, but I imagined it was probably one of the brainier ones in town.

She paused and took another sip of grape juice. "Probably *La Dolce Vita*," she said. "It's an Italian movie directed by a guy named Fellini."

Fellini. That just *sounded* artsy.

"What's it about?" I asked.

"Well, it's partly avant-garde and partly realistic. It's about a guy who wants to be a novelist, but he parties too hard and ends up being a miserable gossip columnist. Some people think it's the best movie ever made."

"Is there any nudity in it?"

"Not really. But it does show a girl getting covered with feathers."

It didn't sound like the most exciting movie in the world, but it certainly sounded artsy. "Can I borrow it?" I asked. She nodded and said she'd bring it the next day. I spent the rest of the afternoon fantasizing about directing my movie, and maybe even becoming a real artsy filmmaker. I could grow a little goatee, drink straight espresso, and travel all over to film festivals and stuff. I'd live in some loft in a big city, not some little suburban dump like

23

Cornersville Trace. That beat the hell out of growing up to be an accountant.

That night, over a dinner that consisted of nothing I can mention in polite company, I asked my father if he knew anything about avant-garde stuff.

"Sure do," he said. "I was in college once, you know."

My mother nodded. "He was, you know, dear."

"My roommate was into avant-garde performance art," he continued. "He used to have me do the technical work when he did shows at the coffee shop."

"What kind of avant-garde stuff did he do?" I asked.

"Well, I remember one time he painted the French flag on his chest and tap-danced while singing 'The Star-Spangled Banner.' While he did that, I used the slide projector to show his old family photos; then he cussed into a microphone for about ten minutes and stood still for half an hour."

"And that was avant-garde?"

"As far as I know. Some people thought it was pretty profound. Never did understand it myself, but I loved working that slide projector. Why do you ask?"

"I'm making a video for my activity period at school, and I want it to be really artsy."

My father's face lit up, as I'd been afraid it would. "Is that the one Max Streich is teaching?" he asked. I forced myself to nod. "Wow, Leon, you're really in for an exciting semester. He's having you guys make health and safety films, right?"

I nodded again, hoping he wouldn't ask what subject I

was doing. My mother tends to get really weird every time I use the word "sex" in front of her.

"That sounds like a very educational class," she said. "Max Streich is such a good teacher, isn't he?"

"I guess so," I said.

Then came the question.

"What's your film going to be about?" my father asked.

"Health stuff," I said.

"Like what? Smoking? Hygiene? Wearing safety goggles?"

"Oh, you know," I said. "Sex, mostly."

My mother, who had been drinking a glass of iced tea, spit half of it out. I should have known better to say anything while my mother was drinking something.

"I don't think that's appropriate for a boy your age," she said as she mopped up the tea.

"Nonsense!" said my father. "He's making an educational film, not a Playboy video!"

I excused myself from the table before I could hear my parents argue about sex any more and ran up to my room. That was about all I wanted my father to know about the project, if I could help it. I knew he would be enthusiastic; he's enthusiastic about every school project I do. But I didn't want him to get too excited or it would ruin the project for me. Worse yet, he might come up with his own ideas and expect me to try them. I had enough ideas of my own.

The more I thought about it, the more the movie was starting to seem like the easiest project in history. For one thing, it sounded like you could do pretty much anything and get away with calling it avant-garde. For another, if my father could work on avant-garde stuff, I was sure I could do it, too. I wasn't necessarily the artsiest guy in town, but I was certainly artsier than he was.

Anna brought *La Dolce Vita* in the next day, and I watched it that night. It was artsy, all right. I could tell it was good, because half the time I had no idea what was going on. It was all in black-and-white, and it opened with a scene where a statue of Jesus is being flown over Rome by a helicopter. Then the main character parties and sleeps with girls who howl at the moon for about three hours, which seems like the sort of life a person would dream of living. Except that he really wants to write a novel, and he keeps getting caught up writing his dumb gossip column, the kind that talks about what movie stars have for lunch, which makes him unhappy, but he keeps doing it because it also makes him rich. Then, at the end, he and all of his famous friends find a giant dead fish on the beach, for some reason. I fast-forwarded through quite a few of the dull parts, but it was still pretty good. And it was exactly what I was looking for.

Right away I started thinking of tons of things I could try to put in the video, but then I got worried that I was letting things get out of hand. I would need a budget of several hundred dollars if I was going to be able to use even half of the scenes I had thought up. And even that wouldn't cover the costs for the scene I had in mind where a statue of a sperm cell is flown over Rome.

So the next morning I was up at six o'clock and ready to head to school. I arrived way before the first bell rang and went to find Mr. Streich already there, talking with Mrs.

Smollet. I hadn't seen her all summer and hadn't bumped into her yet that year. I had forgotten just how frightening she could be. She was one of those people who was probably only about forty but looked sixty-five, with a face like an evil nun's. And she never shut up about moral fiber. She herself, apparently, had moral fiber oozing out of every pore. If it worked like normal fiber, she must have been alarmingly regular.

"It's not wise, Max," she was saying. "I know what these kids are like."

"Oh, come on," said Mr. Streich, who I was glad to see at least wasn't falling for her "kids are evil" routine. "They're good students."

"I'm just warning you, Max," she said, "if you aren't careful, the school could end up getting sued." This was one of her catch-phrases. She was always on the lookout for reasons the school could get sued.

"I'll take my chances," he said, finally looking in my direction. "Hi, Leon," he said.

"Hi," I said, plopping my backpack, which weighed about a ton and a half, onto the ground.

"Well, hi, Leon," said Mrs. Smollet, smiling but sounding about as glad to see me as I was to see her. "How was your summer?"

"Same as any other," I said.

"That's what I was afraid of," she said. And she got up to leave.

"What was that all about?" I asked Mr. Streich as soon as she was out of earshot.

"Well," he said, stretching out and combing his mustache

with his fingers. "You know what she's like. She's not too keen on letting you guys make these videos."

"I'm not surprised," I said. "Based on what she has us do in class, she seems to think that the gifted-pool kids should just be using their gifts to solve crossword puzzles."

He chuckled. "Well, I'm sure she means well." Teachers are never allowed to bad-mouth each other, but you know that half of them probably hate each other. They're just regular people once they get into the teachers' lounge. "I had to do a lot of convincing to get the board to authorize this project in the first place, but I'm sure you're all mature enough to handle it."

"So, anyway," I said, "I've been thinking a lot about my video. I have a lot of ideas already."

"Great!" said Mr. Streich. "I thought you kids . . . er, students might get excited about this project!"

"It's going to be a really artistic film," I said. "I'm thinking of calling it *La Dolce Pubert.*" I pronounced it in such a way as to make it sound as artsy as possible. Like *pyoo-bare*. With the "r" rolling.

He frowned. "Is 'pubert' a word?" he asked. He didn't roll the "r."

"I'm not sure, but it sounds good."

"You might want to look that up before you finish the project."

"I will. Anyway, what I need to know right now," I asked, "is what kind of budget we have to work with."

"Budget?" asked Mr. Streich.

"Yeah," I said. "How much will the school cover?"

"Well," he said, "none."

"None?" I asked.

"None. We have plenty of equipment as it is, unless you want to make explosions. And we can probably find a way to do those with stuff from the lab."

I hadn't thought of explosions before, but it suddenly seemed like a good idea. I'd known the school wasn't going to be willing to pay for a helicopter or anything, but I'd figured we'd have some money for expenses! What were they doing with all our parents' tax dollars? Probably fixing up the stupid gym.

"But I have a lot of ideas for things that we can't do with just the camera and the editing machine!" I said. "How am I supposed to get them to work without a budget?"

"Well," he said, "you might have to scale down your plans a bit. Or, if there are scenes that you absolutely can't do without, I'm sure you can find a way to make it work."

"So what if I can't find a way to do some of the stuff?" I asked.

"Well," he said, smiling, "you'll just have to invent something."

4

The day I turned thirteen, my parents officially began to consider me a rotten teenager.

I had always sort of figured that once I turned thirteen, I'd be treated more like an adult. I mean, I knew I wouldn't be able to buy beer or vote or anything like that; I just thought people might start taking me a bit more seriously. In reality, it turned out to be just the opposite. People occasionally listen to little kids, because they might say something accidentally wise that can be published in one of those stupid gift books that give idiots a warm, fuzzy feeling. You know the kind. They always have all of the writing done in crayon.

However, once you get past twelve, people just look at you like you're about to steal something wherever you go. One time I went into a gas station to buy a can of pop, and the jerk behind the counter got it into his head that I was stealing ice cream. He made me turn out my pockets to show that I didn't have anything frozen in them, like he was a cop in some movie from the thirties and I was a little thief who stole apples from carts. I decided not to buy the pop, and further decided that next time I was out walking around Cedar Avenue with some friends and needed to pee, I'd do it against the wall of the gas station.

Another time, I stopped into a Stationery Limited store in one of the five hundred or so strip malls on Cedar Avenue to buy a pen for some ink drawings I was working on, and the woman gave me the third degree about whether I was using the pen for something legal or for graffiti. I pointed out that I was buying a pen, not a can of spray paint, and that I'd be up there for weeks if I tried to tag a wall with it, but she still took down my name and phone number, which I'm still not sure was even legal. Not that I gave her my real name or anything. I'm nobody's fool.

At home, my father started worrying even more than before about what sort of TV shows I watched. I took to watching certain shows with the remote pointed at the TV, so I could quickly turn it to some educational program—I always knew exactly which ones were on, just in case—if I heard him coming. I'm not sure he really would have believed that I had been watching a show about penguins instead of soft-core porn in the middle of the night, but it was best not to take any chances.

My mother was even worse. When eighth grade started, she decided that I would no longer be permitted to ride the bus. This could be because she has decided I am responsible enough to walk the half-mile to school, which allows me to leave half an hour later since the bus takes so long. In reality, it's because she saw some news story saying that kids as young as twelve are having oral sex on the back of school buses, and she doesn't want me to be a part of it. The whole story was total crap. The worst thing I ever saw happen on the bus was when Ryan Bannon pulled Keith Messersmith's pants down in third grade, and he didn't pull down his under-wear or anything. Besides, if there is actually any fooling around going on in the buses, which I doubt, I want to be there for it.

I've always, however, been allowed to attend major so-cial events, like dances and football games, when I want to. I pass on most of them; the dances are too stupid to bother with, and the food they serve is about as tasty as one of my parents' food disasters. But events that aren't supervised by faculty are always worth checking out, and even though there might be some teachers present at football games, their powers are useless there.

Friday night was the first high school football game of the season, and, though I had no desire to attend it, I knew that the first real party of the year would be at Fat Johnny's Pizza Parlor after the game. Everyone had been making a conscious effort to keep out of trouble the first two weeks of school; it was time for things to start picking up.

Fat Johnny's Pizza Parlor was a pretty decent place; no pizza joint with the word "parlor" in its name can be all that bad. The pizza itself was mostly grease, but it was the last pizza place in town that still had a little video arcade at-tached. Not a big one or anything, just five or six games, plus a pinball machine and a Skee-Ball thing, which was more than most restaurants had. I don't know where the high schoolers went for their parties, but after every football game, people from my class could be counted on to descend on Fat Johnny's like so many locusts.

The games usually ended around ten o'clock, so when ten-thirty rolled around I had my dad give me a ride to the party.

"This isn't going to be too crazy a party, is it, Leon?" he asked. "We're not going to have to pick you up at the police station, are we?"

"It's a pizza place, Dad, not a bar," I said. "I've been here before and never gotten in any trouble." This was only partially true; a couple of times my friends and I had gotten rowdy enough that they'd asked us to leave. This was one of those things my parents just didn't need to know.

"Still, it's a hangout," he said. "A lot of times places like that have trouble with, you know . . . gangs and stuff."

I laughed. "You worry too much, Dad. There aren't any gangs in Cornersville."

Cornersville Trace, which is the official name of our town on all of the maps, though everyone just calls it Cornersville, is a pretty small place. It's big enough to have a mall and everything, but it's just a regular suburb of a fairly small city, not the kind of place where there's a whole lot of gang violence. There are always a handful of kids who seem to *think* they're in gangs, but as far as I can tell, all they ever do is stand around outside the 7-Eleven trying to look tough by giving the finger to people who drive by. If they ever meet a real gang member, I'm pretty sure they'll pee themselves.

As a matter of fact, the worst problems Cornersville really ever has are high schoolers drinking and younger kids adding graffiti to the walls in drainage ditches. But my parents and all their friends are constantly afraid; my dad has even gone so far as to try to invent a security system for the house. The day he installed it, I accidentally opened the door without using the special key he'd given me and was greeted by a siren. The alarm also did something to alert the police, who showed up ten minutes later. Dad explained to them what had happened, and they explained to him that they'd feel a lot better if he just bought a security system instead of building his own, something I'd been trying to tell him the whole time. He listened to them, though.

We pulled into the parking lot, and as I was unbuckling my seat belt, he said, "Now, you know what to do if someone offers you drugs, right?"

"Say 'Thank you very much,' " I said. "Even if it's a kind of drug I already have."

He gave me a glare. "It's just because we love you, Leon."

"I know, Dad. See ya!"

I climbed out and shut the door. According to recent findings, the classic "It's just because we love you" excuse has been in use by parents since the Iron Age, and it's still expected to be the end of the conversation. It doesn't work both ways, though. If I explained that I lied about my middle name because I love them and don't want people to think that they were a couple of kooks who should be sent to parenting skills classes, I'm pretty sure it would get me grounded.

I stepped into Fat Johnny's and saw that it was already full of people from school. A couple of the would-be gangbangers were playing one of the shootout video games, and

Jamie Jenson was cheating at Skee-Ball, standing right at the end of the ramp and putting the balls directly into the fifty hole. Practically every table was full, mostly with people I recognized. I spotted Brian Carlson, the pyro, and Edie Scaduto, the communist, sitting on the same side of a booth, cuddling, which left the other half of the booth open. I took the liberty of sitting there.

"You guys got here fast," I said.

"We snuck out at halftime," said Brian, shaking his head to get his hair out of his face. "The Monks were getting creamed."

"They always get creamed," I said. "I didn't have to show up to see that."

"Smart man," said Brian.

"I approve of football," said Edie. "It's working-class." She was wearing a black turtleneck that matched her dyed-black hair. All together, she looked as though she might be a pitch-black person who'd just had her face dipped in some peach-colored paint.

The only thing most people in the school know about communism is that they're against it. The basic idea behind it is that everyone should share everything and no one should be any richer or poorer than anyone else, which seems okay, except that it works about as well as most of my dad's inventions. As the school's lone commie, Edie approved of all things "working-class" and disapproved of everything she judged to be for the rich. So far that year, she'd disapproved of lacrosse, the mall, name-brand clothing, and school yearbooks. I'm not really sure what she had against yearbooks.

"I didn't think you would approve of football," I said. "It's sort of violent, and to be good at it you have to be freakishly large." She shrugged and went back to kissing Brian's fingers.

A waiter came by and I ordered a Coke. As soon as he was gone, Brian pulled a cigarette lighter out of his pocket.

"I didn't know you smoked," I told him.

"He doesn't," said Edie. "Smoking is one of the ways big business keeps the working class under control."

Brian grinned, picking up a sugar packet and holding it to the flame.

"It just comes in handy now and then," he said. "You never know when you might have to burn something." He set fire to the packet and put it in the ashtray, and we sat watching it burn. The flame worked its way around the edge of the packet before it started to burn the center, and when it did, all the sugar spilled out at once and started to get caught in the flames. It smelled pretty awful.

At any decent restaurant on a normal night, this sort of thing would have gotten us into all sorts of trouble, but in a room full of hyper eighth graders I was sure it was the least of the manager's worries. I looked around and saw that no one was having oral sex on the floor, though. My mother would have been greatly relieved.

"Are you really doing a sex-ed movie?" asked Edie.

I nodded. "An artsy one. Something really avant-garde."

They both nodded; they probably already knew what avante-garde was. Edie probably didn't support it, though.

I hadn't really done much work on it, other than

the mandatory research and discussions about issues that had taken up most of the class time on Wednesday and Thursday. Hearing Mr. Streich say that I would have to invent something had sort of soured me on the whole project. Inventions were my dad's turf—not mine. I did still find myself kicking around the idea of having a good explosion to end the whole thing, though. I couldn't think of a single educational film that wouldn't have been improved by something blowing up. It might not have saved some of the science movies, but it would have helped. Everyone knows that the real point of science class is to blow things up.

Five minutes later, the waiter came back with my Coke, dropped it off at the table, and immediately ran off, looking as though he wished someone would just blow *him* up and get the night over with.

"That poor guy," said Edie, turning away from Brian for the first time that evening to watch the server running toward the back room. "His employer is probably screwing him over." Like most communists, she assumed that just about every worker was getting ripped off somehow.

"Maybe," I said. "Or maybe a roomful of us is more than they trained the poor bastard to handle."

"The poor oppressed workers at Fat Johnny's," said Brian, not sounding too serious. "They should go on strike."

"I doubt they're unionized," I said. "They can't go on a strike."

"Even if they were," said Brian, "could they go on strike to have all middle schoolers banned from the premises? That'd never fly."

"Yeah, but we should really lay off the poor guy. That's probably going to be you or me working that crappy job in three or four years, right?"

"Yeah," said Edie. "Brian, quit burning stuff, okay? We need to be nicer to him."

Brian made a whiny puppy noise, but Edie countered with one of her own and he put the lighter back in his pocket. If there's anything more disgusting than mayonnaise and raisin casserole, it's listening to couples make puppy noises at each other. Even if they're doing it as part of a debate on ethics.

Just as I was about ready to get up and see about wasting a few bucks on pinball, I heard a voice saying "Hey" and turned to see Anna standing next to the booth, wearing a dark blue T-shirt with Kermit the Frog on the front that was at least five sizes too large for her. It hung down to her knees; you couldn't even tell if she was wearing shorts or was naked underneath it or what.

"Have a seat!" I said, sliding down the booth and trying my best not to seem too eager. "This is the best seat in the house if you want to watch Brian and Edie going at it."

"I'm sure I can offer constructive criticism," she said, sitting down and helping herself to a sip of my Coke. As she sat down, her shirt moved just enough that I could see that she did have denim shorts on. I immediately went for another drink myself; putting my lips on the straw was kind of like kissing her, in a secondhand sort of way. This made me feel both excited and rather pathetic at the same time.

"How's your video coming?" she asked me.

"Slowly," I said. "Still kicking around ideas."

"I can help you out on it if you want," she said.

"Sure," I said, "but aren't you busy with your own?"

"No," she said, "I'm finished."

I think all three of the rest of us at the table said "What the hell?" at the same time. The thing had been assigned all of three days ago, we had another month to go on it, and she was already finished?

"I hate your kind," said Brian.

"Overachiever," I muttered.

"Am not," she countered, "it was just really easy. I decided to make it about smoking and drugs at the same time. It was all about how most of the people whose books they make you read in English class were on drugs."

"Poe was into morphine," said Brian.

"Yeah," said Anna. "They think so, anyway. And F. Scott Fitzgerald drank like a sailor on shore leave. Everyone did in those days."

"That's brilliant," I said. "It's history, so they can't tell you that you can't do it."

"Exactly," said Anna. "It's educational about both drugs and literature. They can't complain."

"But you know they will," said Edie with a laugh. "You're supposed to make kids *not* want to take drugs."

"Well, all the people in the movie are dead now," said Anna, "so it's not like it's saying that drugs are healthy. And anyway, most of the kids in school wouldn't read F. Scott Fitzgerald if you put a gun to their heads."

"I'm not sure I'd be able to ready *anything* with a gun to my head," I said.

"We should start a gang," said Anna. "We'll put guns to

people's heads and make them read F. Scott Fitzgerald. If they don't, we'll blow their brains out!"

We all chuckled and continued to hang around, being as nice to the waiter as we could, for a good hour after that. Most of the kids there pretty well ignored us, but I didn't particularly care. I didn't like half of them, and the other half were busy talking about the football game. But the amount of ruckus everyone else was making reassured me that people were ready to raise a bit of the usual hell in class again. As much as the jerks who threw paper around all day bugged me, I had to admit that it had been a boring couple of weeks in class.

Looking around the room, I saw a general scene of pandemonium. Even Joe Griffin, who was sitting at a table with two or three other kids, was grinning like he was up to no good, though I sort of doubted that. Joe Griffin was probably the most religious kid in school, or at least, he tried to act like he was. He was one of those kids who got off on wearing shirts that said stuff like WITHOUT JESUS, THERE'S HELL TO PAY! all the time, and he was always telling people what was and wasn't appropriate and what God thought about abortion, evolution, and Democrats. Even most of the kids who went to church youth groups thought he was sort of a creep. His dad is Gordon Griffin, one of those slimy ambulance-chaser lawyers who advertise on TV that they'll get you a hundred thousand dollars for getting hurt in a car wreck. At Fat Johnny's, though, Joe seemed to have put the angel act to rest for the evening. He'd probably be doing penance the whole rest of the weekend.

As we were getting our bill, Walter Wendt, who was probably the school's biggest football fan, stood up on a table and shouted out, "Monks rule!" It was kind of cool to see that, in his own way, he was just as big a dork as any of us were. It was also fun just to see if the table could hold him; Walter was not a small kid.

"That's funny for so many reasons," said Edie as Walter jumped down.

"Yeah," said Brian. "Seeing as how the Monks suck this year."

"Also, he's Presbyterian," said Edie. "I don't think Presbyterians have monks."

Anna shook her head. "Nope. What the hell kind of name is the Monks, anyway? People probably think we're the Catholic school."

"Well, nobody thinks the San Diego Padres are all Catholic," I said.

"So? They aren't a school. Calling the school football team something religious is way against the law. Church and state are separate."

"Good point," Edie said. "But they'd never manage to change it. All the old ladies in town would picket."

The school wasn't Catholic, but some of the old ladies in town liked to think it was. When Mr. Link got hired as a chemistry teacher the year before, there was a lot of protesting because he was gay. I was convinced that someone had probably told the protesters that, as part of his "homosexual agenda," Mr. Link was planning to teach us to mix up a chemical that would turn us all gay, and further convinced that most of them were dumb enough to believe it. If they were that concerned, there was a Catholic school called St. Julian's right down the road where they could send their kids so they'd be safe from things like gay-inducing chemicals and sex education. Then again, I had a couple of friends at St. Julian's, and their minds were even dirtier than mine.

"You know, I didn't think about that," I said. "I'll bet some people are gonna get really mad about my movie."

"If they even let you show it," said Anna. "Some people get mad that we have sex ed at all. They say it's like giving us a how-to manual."

"Well, I guess if it's avant-garde enough, they won't be able to learn that much," Edie said.

"They wouldn't really learn anything *new*, anyway," said Anna. "The people who complain are just fooling themselves."

Everyone agreed with that. Saying sex ed is giving kids a how-to manual is like saying that showing a cat a Tom and Jerry cartoon will teach them how to chase mice. They already know. If they aren't born knowing, all the other kittens in the pet store will tell them the basics.

The Fat Johnny's manager, a middle-aged guy who looked as though he'd been up for five days straight, shouted that they were closing in fifteen minutes, so we all had to finish up. I'd never seen a manager do that, but having helped cause one to do so made me feel a little guilty. A little proud, but guilty, too.

Brian and I dug in our pockets for cash for the bill, which came to about two bucks. I threw in a couple more for good measure.

"We've gotta tip the guy like crazy," said Edie. "Half the kids here are gonna stiff him."

Anna threw in a five, even though all she had was a sip of my Coke. Edie put in a twenty with the words "Long live the people's revolution" scribbled over the picture on the back. She could afford it; she's all for the working class and all the other commie stuff, but she lives in a huge brick home in Cherrytree Meadows, the gated subdivision near the golf course, and is known to get a huge allowance. When someone calls her on that, she explains that she can't help the fact that her parents are lawyers, but she's planning to move to an organic farm in Oregon as soon as she finishes college.

I started pulling out my phone, and Anna asked what I was doing.

"Calling to get a ride," I said.

"Come on," she said. "You should just walk. I'll go with you."

I was under strict orders not to go for walks in the dark, for one reason or another. But I wasn't about to skip the chance to take a walk with Anna, even if it meant getting disowned and having to live in a foster home. Anyway, if I ended up in one of those, the foster family probably wouldn't have a fit if I had my middle name legally changed to something like Arthur. And the trip was just about half a mile, tops, and all down residential streets. I really didn't think there were any muggers or pedophiles lurking in the bushes of Iris Way. There were still a couple of lawn gnomes on that street that hadn't been stolen, for God's sake.

So I followed her behind Fat Johnny's, through some

split-level house's backyard, and we came out on Garden Way, in the middle of the Flowers' Grove neighborhood. Outside of the particularly wimpy name, I love that neighborhood; it was built during the sixties, during the days of the Space-Age school of suburban design. The houses all have oddly shaped roofs, huge bay windows in the kitchen, and little pods jutting out everywhere. Most of the front doors are on the second story, with stairs leading up to them. And, though you couldn't tell very well in the dark, all the houses are different colors. All the houses in the newer neighborhoods are pretty much white or gray. Yawnsville.

As we got onto the sidewalk, Anna suggested that we play a game of "What Do They Have?" while we walked along.

"How do you play that?" I asked.

"Easy. You look in people's windows and see what they have."

"Sounds slightly illegal," I said.

"Not from the sidewalk," she said, and laughed, making me feel like a real wuss. "If they come out and ask why you're staring at their house, tell them you're studying split-level design in school and you love the eaves on their dormers or something."

"Okay. Let's start." I wondered if we'd see any naked people. I asked if she ever had, and she said, "Nobody you'd want to see naked."

We ran down the sidewalk until we came to a house where the lights inside were on, so we could see in the window.

"These people," I said, "have a very dull living room."

All I could see was a large cabinet full of dishes. Like fancy china dishes.

"Why do people think dishes make great decorations?" asked Anna. "They probably never even use those."

"Yeah," I said. "If they're gonna decorate with dishes, they should at least order some of those commemorative plates with cartoon characters on them."

"Those ones they sell on the Sucker Channel?"

"Right."

We kept walking and saw a house where the people had a chandelier and a table with flowers on it ("People who want you to think they're rich and fancy," Anna decided) and one with an ugly print of a boring painting of lily pads on the wall ("They let the same guy who did the waiting room at the dentist's office do their decorating," I said). But the real score of the game came at a house on the corner of Garden Way and Snapdragon Lane, where the entryway was graced by a very large painting of an old woman who did not look happy in the slightest. As soon as we saw it, we both started cracking up.

"I'll bet it's someone's mother," said Anna. "They probably had it painted from a photo after she died or something."

"They could've picked a photo where she didn't look like she was ticked off," I said. "If I came in the door and saw that, I'd certainly remember to wipe my feet before I stepped on the carpet. I'd be afraid she'd come haunt me if I didn't!"

"At least that's not the worst place they could put it," said Anna. "Think of how it would be to have a picture of their dead mother glaring down at them in bed!"

We laughed so hard at that that we fell into the people's

yard. Then we both thought we heard the door opening and took off running.

My house was only about another block down the road; I was pretty sure that the house was one of the ones I could see from out of my window. We got to my place just a few minutes later.

"Talk to me on Monday," she said. "We'll figure out what we're doing about the video."

"Okay," I said. "Are you sure you'll be okay walking the rest of the way home yourself?"

"Why wouldn't I be?" she asked. I didn't have an answer. So I went up to my door, waved good-bye to her, and stepped inside. It occurred to me about five seconds later that that would have been a perfect time to ask her out, like on a date, but that might've just made things weird. How could I go on working with her on the video if she said no?

However, as it turned out, I didn't have all that long to think about it. As soon as I stepped into the living room, I saw my mother waiting for me. She appeared to be ab-solutely distraught.

"Leon," she said, shaking her head slowly, "you're in big trouble."

"What for?" I asked.

"Remember how you were supposed to call and get a ride from us tonight?"

Oh. That. I had forgotten about that.

"You know perfectly well that you aren't allowed to go for walks after dark," she continued. "And it's after mid-night now. How were we supposed to know where you were?"

"Well," I said, only trying to be helpful, "you could have just called my phone. And anyway, I was never far. If you stood on the porch and shouted, I probably would have heard you."

"Don't smart-mouth me, Leon," she said. "We need to know where you are in case you get in trouble."

"Okay," I said.

"After all, if you get in trouble and we don't know where you are, we can't help you."

"Okay," I said.

"And what if something went wrong here and we needed to get you right away? We wouldn't be able to."

"Okay!" I said a little bit angrily, hoping she would figure out that I already got her point and was being nice enough not to simply give her the finger and walk away. I really hate it when they keep talking after I've gotten the message. But she just glared at me.

"I want you to go talk to your father about this. He's in his workshop."

The workshop was actually the garage. Dad had set up a little lab in there that made it impossible for us to fit two cars in. I walked over to it through the kitchen.

Nothing ever looks like it does in the movies; Dad's lab looks more like a junk shop than a lab. There are no shiny tables, no large flasks full of bubbling pink ooze, and no rats in cages. Just a couple of long card tables covered with assorted gears, bolts, and tools. A person who didn't know that Dad was trying to invent something might see him at work and think he was just building a spice rack, like any normal dad.

When I walked in, he was hunched over one of the tables, screwing something together.

"I heard your mother talking to you," he said, without looking up. "Sounds like you're in the doghouse."

"I was supposed to call and get a ride, but I walked instead. It was only a couple of blocks through Flowers' Grove."

He nodded and looked up. "Well, personally, I don't think it's such a big deal. You weren't anywhere dangerous, as far as I know. But you know the rules."

"Yeah," I said. "Mom said I was supposed to come out here and talk to you."

He put down his gears.

"Well, I guess I'm supposed to punish you, then," he said.

"I guess so."

He turned back around and started tinkering with things again. "Did I tell you what I'm working on now?" he asked.

I groaned as quietly as I could. "Is it the switch to turn off all the electricity?"

I watched him shake his head from behind. "Letting that one slide for a while, Leon. I got a better idea."

"Something for the world of accountants?"

"Not yet, but I'll get to that. I'm going for a novelty for now."

"A novelty?"

"A novelty. Something that'll make me rich enough to buy a bigger lab and be able to concentrate all my efforts on inventing a kind of pen that will just disintegrate when it runs out of ink, which is the invention that will revolutionize accounting."

"So," I asked, "what kind of novelty are you working on?"

"A special kind of matchstick," he said. "This kind will light itself at the sound of someone snapping their fingers."

Now, that, I had to admit, was pretty cool.

"How would it work?" I asked.

"Well, that's the tricky part," he replied. "There are lots of ways to make matches. They used to be made by adding phosphorous to the tip of a stick, but that killed an awful lot of factory workers. Now they use lots of different stuff. I think. Anyway, it'll work sort of like the Clapper, that thing that lets you turn lights off and on by clapping. Only without having to plug it in."

"How are you going to manage it?"

"Oh, I have some ideas," he said, "involving wires and some chemicals and stuff that'll react to sound waves. There's a lot of math involved—but that'll give me something to do at the office when things are slow."

I'd been in Dad's office, a little joint near the mall called Heimlich and Robbins or something, a couple of times. I privately referred to it as the Boredom Factory. It was staffed by a bunch of men who wore bow ties and enormous glasses and annoying women who actually bought those books of wise things kids said with all the writing in crayon.

"So," he continued, "I've made a little bit of progress so far. I just need to find ways to make it a lot less dangerous. And, as part of your punishment, you're going to be helping me on Monday night."

"Deal," I said.

"And," he said, "you're also going to help your mother

cook dinner before that. But I was going to make you do that anyway, so it's not really a part of your punishment."

I nodded and headed upstairs to my room and lay down in my bed, hoping to get the night over with. I let everything from the day run through my head. Self-lighting matches. The Monks. Anna walking away from the house alone in the dark and not caring, not even worrying that she might get in trouble, since her parents trusted her. All the faces of the kids from Fat Johnny's. Wendt on the table. Edie and Brian making out. Anna grabbing my Coke. Jamie cheating at Skee-Ball. I tried to remember everything everyone had said. Pretty soon it felt almost like I was in a trance, and I thought maybe if I concentrated hard enough, I might be able to have one of those out-of-body experiences where you turn into a ghost and float around a bit, with your body still lying in bed. If that happened, I'd float over to Anna's house and take her by surprise, assuming that having ghosts show up wasn't a regular occurrence at her house. But both of us—me and my ghost, if I had one—stayed put.

Anna once told me that the word for the state of being not quite awake but not quite asleep is "hypnogogic." That's what I was, lying in bed that night. Hypnogogic. I was awake but still having dreams. After the images of the pizza place faded, there were dreams about the old woman in the painting, who all of a sudden scared the crap out of me. In the dreams, she was following me around with that pissed-off look on her face, haunting me as punishment for laughing at her. Eventually I forced myself to get out of bed, looked out the window, and tried to see if I could find the house where the painting was. I know it's stupid, but I was very relieved when I didn't see it.

So, feeling a little less frightened, I got back into bed and fell asleep. Not just half asleep, but really asleep.

The dreams were better that way. One of them was about Anna.

5

There's this feeling I always get on Saturday afternoons, sitting around in the living room, watching the dust blow around in the sunlight that beams in through the blinds. Like there's nothing going on, and I ought to be bored, but I'm just not, and things are only going to get better over the next day or so. Like being excited and bored at the same time. I don't think there's a word for it. At least, not in English. Maybe they have one in Japanese.

After I woke up I watched TV for as long as I could stand it, which, on Saturday afternoon, wasn't all that long. There wasn't much on besides golf tournaments, and I think you have to be in a coma to watch golf on television. You might just as well watch people knitting. Actually, if people used those knitting needles as swords in between working on pot holders, knitting might be a good thing to see on TV. A little violence can go a long way; imagine how much more fun figure skating could be if they had two figure skaters duking it out on the ice. Combat figure skating. I'd watch that.

Still, bad TV or not, I never did venture out of the house, not for the whole weekend. Since the first two weeks of school were over, the unofficial grace period had passed and teachers would be giving homework right and left. I knew I had to relax while I still had the chance.

By eight-thirty on Monday, it was quite apparent that everyone else knew that the year had started in earnest, too. When the principal went on the intercom to lead us in the Pledge of Allegiance, I noticed that a bunch of people were saying joke pledges, like "one nation, under pants, in the vestibule, with silky see-through garters for all."

That was just the start. By the end of homeroom, it was clear that the whole "well-behaved" facade was over. Jerks were throwing paper around and thinking it was the funniest damn thing ever. Kids were having contests to see who could say "penis" the loudest without getting caught by the teacher. Danny Nelson was going around with a clipboard, collecting money and laying two-to-one odds that Nick Malley and Jenny Levin would be broken up by the end of the week. Classes were loud and obnoxious, and the general attitude was not one of maturity. As much as all the jerks in class drove me crazy from time to time, it was good to know they hadn't all gone soft.

I had this guy named Coach Wilkins for history. Now, it was a strict rule of mine never to trust a man who insisted on being called "Coach," but at least Wilkins knew his stuff, and he really got into his history lectures. Watching him teach was like watching a preacher on one of those Christian

Big Hair channels. He'd get all excited, shouting and waving his hands around and even jumping up and down when the mood struck him. I wasn't sure what exactly he coached.

"People in the 1830s believed that it was America's destiny to expand all the way to the Pacific Ocean!" he shouted. "Can anyone tell me what the name of this concept was?"

"Manifest Destiny," someone muttered.

"Manifest Destiny!" he roared, raising his fist in the air like he was imitating either the Statue of Liberty or Malcolm X. "Expand America's territory all the way to the Pacific Ocean!" He pounded his fist hard on his desk for each of the last few words; he did that so often that it was a miracle his desk hadn't cracked. I suppose we were lucky that he wasn't teaching in some sort of costume, though I figured that that couldn't be far off. I'm not sure what movie it was that convinced teachers that dressing up like a cowboy made you a great teacher, but more than one had tried it over the years. One had even stopped calling us students and started calling us "varmints." Even after he stopped wearing the costume.

Had he been alive during the Revolutionary War, I'm sure Wilkins would have been the guy grabbing his musket and running toward the British army screaming, like he was having the time of his life, while everyone else was marching in formation. Then, when they were all huddled around the fire, tending their wounds and trying not to starve or freeze to death, he would have been saying, "Come on, you guys! Let's all sing 'Yankee Doodle' for the three hundredth time!" He would probably have been hanged from the highest tree early on. I pictured this series of events in my mind fairly often; maybe after *La Dolce Pubert* I could make a movie called *Wilkins Goes to War*. Or maybe *The Road to Cornersville*, like all those war movies with Bob Hope that my grandfather has on video.

I didn't really go in for the paper-throwing or "penis"-shouting matches, but I still sat in the back row. Everyone knows that not only are classes more exciting in the back row, but the back row is also better for grabbing a nap or for working on a drawing instead of taking notes, which is what I was doing. I had this great thing going where every few classes I'd do a drawing in the top corner of a sheet of notebook paper, and some of them weren't half bad. I had a good drawing of a knight on a mountain and one of the back of a guy's head, as he was staring down a road at a UFO. Every now and then I'd fantasize about collecting all of them into a book called *Corner Drawings* that could maybe set the art world on fire.

About midway through class, Coach Wilkins looked up and noticed that there were a handful of students in the front couple of rows and the rest of us were in the back. The middle rows were like a little gulf of empty desks.

"Can all of you in the back move up a few rows, please?" he asked. "I'd like to have everyone sitting up close."

"It's Manifest Destiny!" I shouted, raising my fist toward the ceiling. "We're going to expand our classroom all the way to the back wall!"

You don't have to be smart to be a smartass. But it helps.

He stared at me for a couple of minutes. Well, it seemed like a couple of minutes. It was probably just a couple of seconds.

"Well," he said, "at least you're paying attention."

I wasn't really.

When my corner drawing—a Picasso-style abstract portrait of a cowboy—was finished, I started scribbling down ideas for the video. We were all supposed to turn in outlines of our movies in activity period the next day. I knew I wasn't going to be able to manage the whole "sperm cell flying over Rome" sort of thing, but there was a lot I could still probably do on no real budget. Pretty soon, I had it together.

The opening would be a whole bunch of pictures of famous paintings of naked people, along with a whole bunch of weird stuff that didn't seem to make sense. Like if I showed a bunch of tadpoles swimming around. It would seem weird, but then someone might notice that tadpoles looked sort of like sperm, which would make it all make sense. Sort of.

There would be rock music in the background the whole time, plus a narration about how everyone changes, everyone thinks about sex, everyone jacks off, and it's all totally normal, even if the movie itself wasn't normal at all. That was a nice touch, I thought. Having the movie not be normal to show kids that they were. Then, of course, I would end it with a kiss scene, then an explosion. Avant-garde art was always showing things like that—an act of love followed by an act of pure destruction. It made some sort of point.

Yeah, that looked like a pretty good start to me. I knew I would have to find ways to get a bit odder, and maybe a bit more explicit, but I was off to a good start. I would still have to write a script for voice-overs. I was relying on the fact that Mr. Streich had said we could find a way to blow something up to get the explosion in there. That was really the make-or-break moment of the film, the ending that would determine whether the kids who saw it cheered and clapped or just said, "Well, the nudity was okay."

I finished off the rest of my morning by scribbling, in letters too tiny and light to be visible to the naked eye, "Anna likes Leon. . . . Anna: Ask Leon out . . . ," and trying to send a psychic message in her direction, which I knew wouldn't work, but which certainly couldn't hurt anything.

At lunch I wandered over to the table where Anna and most of the rest of the advanced studies gang was sitting. If she was going to follow my psychic advice, she didn't indicate it at all when I sat down. She just said "Hey."

James Cole, the French-speaking pot smoker, was wearing sunglasses, probably trying to cover up having been stoned or wasted the night before. Or maybe he'd been stoned a month earlier and was afraid that it might still be showing. "*Bonjour,* assmonkey," he said. I knew he didn't mean any offense; it seemed like he came up with a different thing to call people every Monday. "Assmonkey" was just his vocabulary word of the week.

"Voltaire was the best French-language playwright of the eighteenth century," said Dustin Eddlebeck. James shrugged. He had learned French as a toddler, when his dad was stationed in the south of France; just because he spoke French didn't mean he went around reading French plays all the time.

"Voltaire's plays sucked," said Anna, who should know, what with her parents being scholars of the era and all.

"Maybe," said Dustin, "but they had a lot of sex in them, right?"

"Not really. You should read some of them," said Anna.

"There's sex in them," he maintained. "You just have to read between the lines." Dustin would not be satisfied until he'd read every sex scene in classical literature, and he was pretty sure that just about every character in every classic book was having sex with every other character if you read between the lines—the writers just had to be sneaky about it in the old days.

Now, I don't wish to imply that I don't care about sex or that I don't think about it; hell, if I dedicated all the time I spent thinking about sex to working on, say, learning to speak Italian, I would have been fluent by the end of seventh grade.

Dustin Eddlebeck, however, was just plain sick. In seventh grade, part of sex ed was showing us a video of a baby being born, and though this indeed meant seeing actual nudity in the classroom, and I'm talking full-on shots of parts you don't normally even see in *Playboy*, it was entirely too disgusting to be arousing. However, whenever they show that sort of thing, there's always one kid who sits there grinning and going, "Whoa, mama!" or something like that. Dustin Eddlebeck was that kid. You could show him a picture of a shaved camel and it would turn him on, if he had ever been turned off to begin with. Which I doubt.

Brian slid into the seat right next to Edie and flipped his hair out of his eyes.

"I think I might get to see Dr. Guff today," he said, smiling. "Coach Hummel caught me drawing band logos on my jeans with a permanant marker and said he was going to recommend that I get counseling." Brian's jeans were regularly decorated with logos of every metal band known to man.

"He's probably just joshing you," said James.

"Yeah," said Brian. "But I can dream."

A couple of people from the gifted pool had been sent to talk to Dr. Guff, the school shrink, for one reason or another, and they'd all come back with wild stories about what they'd told him. James Cole swore that he answered every question by singing a few bars of "Alice's Restaurant," by Arlo Guthrie, which I'd never heard, though Anna told me she'd play it for me sometime. Dustin saw Dr. Guff once and claimed to have told him he'd lost his virginity at nine to a female truck driver in South Bend, Indiana.

Personally, I wasn't sure whether to believe a word of it—no one knew much about Dr. Guff, not even where his office was, and there were no pictures of him. I couldn't find a single mention of him on the Internet. I sort of suspected that he might just be a legend, like Bigfoot or the giant mutant spider some kids in my first-grade class claimed to have found in a drainage ditch one day.

Whether these stories were true was irrelevant; we spent lots of time thinking of funny things to say to Dr. Guff, like claiming that we were pretty sure that our parents were cantaloupes or that we thought God was a space alien.

Anna turned to me and said, "Do you have your outline for the video ready yet?"

"You bet," I said. I dug it out of my backpack and handed it to her. She looked at it critically.

"This is a good start," she said. "But you should really have some people painting each other with their tongues."

"Can we work that in?"

"Maybe. And let's lose the tadpoles—the sperm symbolism is too obvious."

Dustin Eddlebeck looked up from his lunch. "Hey, wait a minute," he said. "Are you guys doing the sex-ed video together?"

I stopped myself from blushing, which took a great deal of effort. "Well, sort of," I said.

"I'm letting him use some of my parents' equipment," said Anna, doing a good job of covering things up. If word got around that we were doing the video together, we'd never hear the end of it. Ever. It was good to know that she recognized this and didn't want to deal with it, either.

I turned back to Anna and said, a little more quietly, "So when should we get going on it?"

She took a sip of her Coke. "What are you doing tonight?" she asked.

"I've gotta stay home," I grumbled. "I have to help my mother cook dinner, then help my dad in his . . . garage." I was going to say I was working on an invention with him but decided against it. Better not to dwell on these things.

"How about tomorrow?" she said. "Wanna come over to my place? We can dig through my parents' books and look for ideas."

"Sure," I said. Across the table, Dustin fixed me with a goofy grin, as though I'd just been invited to go over to her place to have a shower with her or something. Not that I didn't wish I had been. But I gave Dustin a look back indicating that I would have no problem with hiring a couple of the football players to kill him. There were plenty who were just smart enough to know that their best chance for the future was a career as a hired goon.

"Hey, Leon," Brian, who was a few chairs down, chimed in. "I keep forgetting to ask you . . . did you ever hook up all those speakers?"

"Crap! I forgot to tell you guys!" I said. "I hooked them up last weekend."

"Did you have a whole wall?"

"Just about half, but it was a start." Everyone had leaned in; this project had taken up discussion time every day at the table the year before, and now that I was getting to the story of how it came out, I had everyone's full attention.

"You used AC/DC, right?" asked James.

"Yeah."

"Well, come on! Did it work?"

"Yeah, for about one second. Then I blew a fuse."

"But how did it sound for that one second?" asked Dustin.

I smiled. "It was the loudest thing you ever heard," I said. "If I'd finished the song, my family probably would have been kicked out of town."

"Rock 'n' roll, my friend," said Dustin. "Rock 'n' roll."

"Holy corn bread," said James, resurrecting one of his favorite expressions from the year before. "That must've kicked ass!"

"Dude," said Brian, shaking some of his hair out of his face and starting to get worked up, "all you need are some resistors, and a couple of potentiometers, maybe." He started getting really into it, spouting off a bunch of technical stuff that might as well have been Greek. You could tell he was getting excited, because without even thinking about it, he'd pulled out his lighter and was flipping it around in his fingers.

Brian was one of those mechanical-type kids who were always getting stuff at Radio Shack to make their flashlights bright enough to blind their enemies or something like that. I was convinced that if he died in school, it would be from holding a minifan he'd modified to spin so fast that it lifted him off the ground, causing him to fly through the ceiling headfirst. But I was also convinced that there were few more memorable ways to die. It should go without saying that a kid who is into both mechanical things and fire is destined to do great things.

There must be one of those kids in every advanced studies class, because in seventh grade Mrs. Smollet gave him some information about some camp for kids like him. The top of the flyer said, "Do you always have to know how things work? Do you have a tendency to tinker?" Any teacher who thinks it's wise to give a kid a flyer that asks him if he has a "tendency to tinker" should be fired in a large public assembly. In any case, Brian passed on the camp.

By the end of lunch I was on enough of a high to get through the rest of my day without too much trouble. Even though I wasn't entirely sure what Brian was talking about with all the gears and stuff, just hearing him yammering on made me excited about trying to get the wall of sound working again, and the video was starting to feel like it was back on track. Not to mention that I had an invitation to go over to Anna's house the next day. With all those things, I had enough going on in my head to sit around pretending to be taking notes while I was actually drawing up plans for the wall of sound or writing down more movie ideas. It was al-most enough to make me forget all about the hell that surely awaited me at home that night, cooking and inventing.

Almost.

6

Most of the cookbooks in my parents' collections aren't really cookbooks so much as advertisements. Like, Crisco put out whole cookbooks in which every recipe called for an obscene amount of "Crisco® Brand Shortening." The idea behind it was that if people kept cooking things out of the books, they'd run out of Crisco faster and have to buy more of it. That's all very well and good, but the problem is, a lot of products can't really be made into all that much stuff, so the people writing the cookbooks really had to stretch for ideas after the third or fourth recipe. I hope against hope that they didn't really expect people to eat some of the recipes they came up with; they were just doing their job, coming up with as many ideas as they could. They probably didn't count on people like my parents.

I was able to hang out in my room for a couple of hours after school, poking around with the wires on the speakers to see if anything was broken or burned all to hell, and trying to get them back into shape instead of being a tangled mess, which they seemed to have become all by themselves. Then, just as the clock struck six, I was called downstairs.

My mother was dressed in one of her food disaster costumes, which she only wore on special occasions, when she was really trying to make cooking into a chance to spend quality time with my dad and me. On these occasions, when she cooked one of the horrible meals, she liked to dress up like a housewife from whatever decade the cookbook of the night came from. Tonight she was dressed in a costume from the 1950s, with a long dress and a yellow apron, and she was wearing hideous, pointy red eyeglasses. I was convinced that this did not make the meals any more edible, and further convinced that anyone who was into women's rights would consider the whole scene a giant step backward. But, as usual, I kept my mouth shut. I was under punishment, after all. And, anyway, it could have been worse. The outfit she wore when she used a cookbook from the seventies could probably cause blindness if one looked directly at it. My dad's costumes, at least, weren't so bad. Men's fashions have remained pretty much stagnant, just a plain shirt and tie, for decades now.

"What are we making tonight, then?" I asked.

"Applesauce casserole with green beans," she said, grinning evilly. "It'll get you every vitamin you need for sure, because all the fruits and vegetables are mixed together in the same dish!" I silently wondered whether putting the two categories in the same dish would actually cause them to sort of cancel each other out.

"Here," she said, handing me an apron of my own. "Put

this on." When I did, I realized that it had the words KISS THE COOK printed on the chest. I hoped she wouldn't try to follow those directions.

She handed me a copy of a slim, stapled-together cookbook called *Everyday Is Applesauce Day*, and I flipped through it for a bit, feeling bad for the poor guys who were told to come up with a whole bunch of things that could be made out of applesauce. There's really only one thing you can make out of applesauce, and that's, well, applesauce.

My first job was to mix up the applesauce with milk, green beans, assorted spices, and a couple of eggs in a large bowl. I started out just stirring it like I would normally stir something, but Mom stopped me.

"That's not the right way to do it," she said.

"What do you mean?" I asked. "I'm stirring, aren't I?" Honestly, there are times when I think they don't think I can do anything right.

"Yes," she said, "but you're not following the rules. When you cook a food disaster, you have to pretend it's the nineteen fifties, or whatever decade the cookbook was printed. You can pretend you're a fifties teen."

My mother was not above forcing quality time on me.

I dropped the spoon into the dish and started to walk off, combing my hair with my fingers.

"Where are you going?" she called as I walked down the hall toward the front door.

"Out to Dead Man's Curve," I said. "My friends and I are gonna listen to some rock 'n' roll, do some drag racing, and maybe have a knife fight. We're rebels."

"Nice try, Leon," she said. "Get back here." I had expected her to call me on that one, but surely she couldn't blame me for trying. "Just talk about Eisenhower or something while you stir."

I gulped and silently thanked God that none of my friends were present to witness the whole thing, then started to stir and say "That President Eisenhower sure is swell" and things like that. While she got the oven ready and mixed up the pastry top for the casserole, she said things like, "Now, I was talking to Betty next door, and she said that if you mix green beans into things, it'll give your children more iron. Do you think you're getting enough iron, dear?"

"Gee, Mom," I said, "I sure hope so. I'm gonna need to be strong when the Russians attack us!"

"Oh, don't you worry about that, dearest," she said. "You just worry about what all of those friends of yours have been doing at the drive-in. I don't want you getting into that kind of trouble! You keep your hands to yourself, mister."

I almost stopped stirring as I realized that, in a completely sneaky way, my mother had just given me a sex talk.

If that's what the fifties were like, and, in particular, if these recipes were really what the food was like, it's a wonder anyone survived them at all. The suicide rate was probably through the roof.

But I managed to steer the conversation far away from sex by talking about hula hoops and integrating schools. By the end of the whole thing, I was actually sort of getting into pretending to be a rebellious fifties teen. This, in particular, made me want to stick my head in the oven.

Half an hour later, we put the food on the table, and my dad sat down, looked at the cookbook, and said, "Oh, boy! I was waiting for Applesauce Day!"

"I'm pissed off," I said. "I can't believe I had to go to school on Applesauce Day!"

"Leon, watch your language," said my mother. So much for playing along. I didn't think "pissed" was a cuss word to begin with. My mother lived in fear of cuss words; the very mention of the infamous "f-word" would cause her eyes to bug out, unless it was being said by someone with a British accent. For some reason, she found it less offensive coming from the British.

The food itself could have been a whole lot worse, I suppose. You couldn't really taste the green beans all that well; it wound up just tasting like a whole plateful of hot, chunky applesauce. This was a relief, but it looked gross and I still had to endure the lame jokes my parents made about it.

"Boy!" said my father. "Can't you just taste that iron, Leon?"

"It does taste kind of like metal," I said.

"He stirred the applesauce and green beans all by himself," said my mother, as though this was the big deal of the year or something. "We're going to have to start punishing you more often, Leon!" A decade of formal education and they were proud that I could stir.

I positively shoveled the last bit of applesauce into my mouth to make sure I didn't have to answer right away. By the time I'd swallowed it, I didn't have to say anything, because my father was making comments about how the colors made it look like some sort of junk you could spread in your garden to make the roses look brighter. That was probably a better use for it than to eat it for dinner. Even if it wasn't as horrible as most of the food disasters, it wasn't exactly a satisfying meal. Applesauce is a side dish, not a main course. After I was finished, I was still pretty hungry. Call me a spoiled brat if you must, but being chock-full of iron didn't really make me any less hungry.

After dinner I sort of felt like a prisoner who had just eaten his last meal before being executed, with a couple of key differences. Number one, criminals get to request whatever they want for their last meal. I sincerely doubt that any criminal has ever asked for applesauce with green beans in it. Number two, going out to the garage to help Dad find a way to make matches respond to a finger-snapping sound wasn't exactly the same thing as being executed. This is not to say that it was pleasant, but at least I had a better than average chance of surviving, provided that I kept my wits about me and didn't blow myself up.

After I cleared my plate, I tried to buy myself some time by going into the living room and turning on the television, flipping from one prime-time sitcom to another. Sometimes if you look busy, people will give you a few minutes, even if you're just watching something stupid on TV. Did you ever notice how many sitcom families have pretty much the same living room, only with slightly different decorations? The front door opens right into the living room, and there's usually a staircase behind the couch. I don't know anyone who's right inside their living room when they open the front door; this is just one of many reasons that sitcoms are pretty much pure crap.

Anyway, this didn't last very long. After about five minutes, my mother came in and told me it was time to go to the workshop. I walked toward the door to the garage, pretending I was about to face a firing squad. They would ask me for my last request, and I'd say that I wanted a bulletproof vest, and then I'd wink and give the onlookers a sly smile. Well, not really. If I was about to get shot, I'd probably just whimper and crap my pants. But since I knew I wasn't going to get shot, no matter what went wrong with the inventing, I was able to keep control of my various functions.

When I stepped into the garage, Dad was already there, wearing a white lab coat, which was just plain embarrassing to see. I was convinced that no real inventors actually wore those and was equally convinced that there was no point at all in wearing one when there were no other inventors around to impress.

"Hiya, Leon," said my dad, grinning so enormously that I thought he would probably be sore in the morning. "All set?"

"I guess so," I said, pulling out one of the stools and having a seat. "What would you like me to do?"

"First, put this on." He held up a long white lab coat and, to my complete horror, handed it to me. I put it on, thanking heaven that the garage door was closed.

He handed me a notebook. "Mostly just take notes for me. That'll be a big help." I pulled the stool a little closer to the table where Dad had all of his chemicals and junk sitting out. "I'll call out some numbers and names of chemicals, and you just write down what I tell you."

I opened up the notebook, flipped to the first blank page, and got ready.

"Test number one," he said. "One milligram of boron." I wrote that down; then he said a few more chemicals and mentioned mixing them over flame until they reached the boiling point. Then he did just that, putting them all together into a beaker, putting the beaker over a hot plate, and stirring them while they got hotter. He got the weirdest look on his face while he did it, like some sort of mad scientist. I wasn't sure he was actually much of a scientist, but he was certainly mad.

When it was boiling, he poured it all into some water ("dilute in one liter of H_2O," as I wrote in my notes) and said, "Now we just wait for it cool down."

The mixture he had made was an ugly blue thing, like the disinfectant people at hair salons keep combs in.

"So that's the stuff?" I asked. "Is it going to catch fire on command?"

"Well, not on its own. But it's fairly flammable. . . . Every match will have a tiny power source in it, and some gizmos that are sensitive to noise. It's pretty complicated. I've got the things rigged up to ignite, just a bit, when they hear the noise, but the trick is to make the chemical coating of the match flammable enough to catch fire without being so flammable that it's dangerous."

This struck me as a little unwise. Wouldn't the sound of a snap set off every match in the matchbook at once? And what about similar sounds, like drumbeats? A guy at a rock concert could set his jacket on fire in a real hurry. But I didn't say any of that out loud.

"How much do you think they'll cost?" I asked.

"Well, they're novelty matches, not normal ones," he said. "So I think people will be willing to pay extra for them."

He hadn't exactly answered my question; I guessed that the matches would probably cost so much that no one would be able to afford a single book of them, and was sure that anyone dumb enough to go into hock for a novelty product was probably not smart enough to take all the necessary safety precautions. On the plus side, having matches that could be lit accidentally would be a great way for someone—Brian Carlson, for instance—to say that he honestly hadn't *meant* to burn the school down; the matches had just gone off by themselves.

Just about then, the door opened, and my mother stepped into the garage. "I want a picture of this," she said, holding up her camera. "My two inventors, hard at work."

I knew better than to complain but briefly wondered if it would be worth it to drink some of the blue flammable junk to see if it killed me, which it surely would have done. I decided against it, and she had us stand there, both of us in lab coats, and she took a picture. I felt like a first-class ding-dong. If the invention turned out to be a success, the picture would probably be published in *Inventor's Digest* or something. Luckily, I didn't think it would be any more successful than the rest of Dad's inventions, so I didn't have much to worry about.

Finally, the mixture for the test was cooled, and Dad was ready to try it out. By that time, it had cooled into a somewhat more solid mixture, like blue clay. It looked sort of like how I imagined plastic explosives to look, and I guess that's what it was, in a way.

"Keep the notebook ready," he said. "Write down everything that happens in the test. The real key is going to be absolute precision in the amount of mixture used per match."

He picked up a plain little stick of wood, on which there was a tiny metal device of some sort, and put it on a digital scale. I wrote down its weight. Then, using some piece of goofy gear that looked about like a turkey baster, he added a drop of the blue stuff to the end, covering the metal device, and then held it for a moment, waiting for it to dry. Once it seemed solid, he put it on the scale again and had me write down the new weight.

"Now," he said, "when I subtract the first measurement from the second one, I'll know exactly how much of the material is on the match."

"Makes sense," I said. "Are you going to test it?"

He smiled, held up the match with one hand, and snapped his fingers with the other one.

I looked at the match and was not at all surprised when nothing happened.

Dad, however, frowned, and snapped harder. That time, there was a tiny spark, but nothing caught fire.

"I guess it's not so flammable that it's dangerous," I said.

Dad just stared for a second. "Damn," he said.

"Time to try a new mixture?"

Dad just sat there, looking bummed out.

"Well," he said, finally, "I know what I'd do if I were Thomas Edison."

"What?"

"I'd hire somebody to invent it for me and then take all the credit. That's what he did with the lightbulb, film projectors, and everything else he ever made. I'm just lucky he's too dead to steal this one from me."

Then he had me help him clean the place up.

As much as I disliked all the invention junk, I couldn't help feeling sorry for the poor guy. I thought about how long it might take him to get the mixture to do what he wanted at this rate, which was a very, very long time. The thought of him spending most of his life in the garage trying to make something that, if it worked, couldn't possibly be safe enough to sell in stores was just plain sad.

7

Tuesday seemed like it would be a good day in school. Not only did I have the advanced studies thing in the morning, but instead of being in class the last forty-five minutes of the day, I had the first weekly gifted-pool meeting, where we'd all meet with Mrs. Smollet in the special classroom that had couches and stuff. Going there didn't do a whole lot to make you popular among other kids, but all you had to say was that you just went because it got you out of class and nobody really held it against you. Also, most of the kids in school knew that half of the people there were, as I have said, a bunch of troublemakers, and it was rumored that Mrs. Smollet tried to have us all expelled pretty regularly.

I almost didn't blame her; we did our best to make life difficult for her, though she didn't always notice. When she had us do a thing in seventh grade where we were supposed to bring in our favorite poem, we all tried to outdo each other finding the worst poem imaginable, and she didn't quite catch on. She said that the one James read about how "it takes a heap o' livin' to make a house a home" brought tears to her eyes. And not because it sucked. And that was one of our minor stunts; the best reactions usually came when we pretended to be devil worshippers.

Tuesday was also the day I was going over to Anna's house, which made it doubly exciting. In the morning I took a shower about twice as long as the ones I normally take, brushed my teeth twice, and used a hair dryer to get my hair to look its best, even though on the best days it tends to look like a disaster by noon. I tried some hair spray and hoped for the best.

Dad was already out the door, on his way to the Boredom Factory, when I left, but Mom was in the kitchen, unloading the dishwasher. "I won't be home right after school today," I told her. "I'm going over to a friend's house to work on the video." I wouldn't have told her that the friend was Anna if she offered never to cook a disaster for dinner again; I could just imagine the look on her face if I did.

"Okay," she said. "Just make sure you come back before dark."

"I'll call you if I'll be any later than that," I promised, though I knew it would probably slip my mind. Could I actually be at Anna's that long? What could we do that would take us till dark? Well, I had a few ideas, but none that I actually expected to happen.

So I hiked off to school, wishing that I was on the bus, in a way. But if I was, I would have had to leave about half an hour earlier, and instead of sitting in the back watching all the kids having oral sex (which they weren't doing anyway), I probably would have been assigned to sit by one of those assholes who thinks he's a big deal because he's a third-string defensive back on the football team.

That had happened the year before; instead of getting to sit wherever I wanted, I had to sit next to Nick Norton, who spent most of his time trying to get me to do his damn homework for him, or at least to let him copy mine. That was usually pretty easy to get out of, though, since I hadn't done it myself. Anyway, I was glad to be rid of jerks like him, at least on the bus. I still had to deal with them most of the rest of the day.

I got to school with just about five minutes to spare and walked into the media immersion room, where everybody was sitting in the circle already. I took a seat next to Anna, trying to look all casual and stuff, like the fact that I was going over to her place that afternoon was no big deal.

"So," I said, just muttering instead of actually talking, "you wanna just meet up after school and walk to your place? Or do you ride the bus home?"

"We can walk," she said. "They won't let people on the bus if they don't ride it normally anymore. Some kind of security threat."

"Well, that makes sense," I said. "How do you know some kid isn't going to another kid's house to plot a killing spree or something? There are so many terrorists in Cornersville."

"At least we don't have to go through metal detectors to get into the school building," said Anna. "Not yet, anyway."

Our parents were always coming up with new and exciting ways to keep us safe; a few had suggested that they put metal detectors in all the buildings. Others had said we should all have clear plastic backpacks, which struck me as dumb; any kid with half a brain could still hide something in his lunch bag.

"Did you finish your outline?" Anna asked.

I nodded.

"Same here," she said. "Check this out."

She handed me a piece of paper. It said:

Anna Brandenburg
Smoking/Drugs Video Synopsis

My video will consist of a series of images of dead people, with voice-overs saying which drugs they took, followed by the message that kids should avoid drugs and smoking if they don't want to end up as dead as the people in the movie.

"You're sort of glossing over a few key points," I said. "Like who the dead people are going to be."

"I'll plead ignorance. It's easier to get excused for something after you've already done it than to ask permission beforehand, right?"

Mr. Streich came waltzing on in just as the bell rang, and clapped his hands together once or twice to get our attention. "Okay, gang," he said, like calling us a gang would make us think he was any cooler than he was. "Everybody got their outlines ready to go?"

We all pulled them out and Mr. Streich began to walk around the room, looking them over. This whole process struck me as slightly backward. We'd done a bit of brain-storming and some talk about what was expected of us and all that, but we were also supposed to spend at least another week on research before we started making the videos. It seemed to me that it would be a better idea to do the research before we started in on the outlines. But that's just me. I honestly think they if they just let the gifted pool run things, the school would be in better hands. And anyway, I couldn't complain. I wanted to get started on the video, not spend all my time reading books from the health section.

Mr. Streich looked over Anna's outline for a good long time. "Well," he said, "this is a little morbid. Do you think you could also add some instructional things, like how to resist the pressure to smoke and take drugs?"

"I will consider it with great care over the coming weeks," said Anna. She didn't say that she'd already finished the video.

Mr. Streich moved on to mine and stared down at it.

"Oh," he said, as he got to the end, "I forgot to tell you something. I know I said we could find a way to put in an explosion, but I talked to some people in the office about it, and they said I couldn't allow that. I can't let you do anything dangerous."

I was starting to get pissed off already—and it was too early to be all that pissed. If I was angry before regular classes even started, I'd never make it all the way through the day. "What if I didn't make the explosion myself?" I asked. "What if I just used some footage of an explosion that somebody else filmed?"

"I'll ask, but I doubt it. If you show anything with a lot

79

of fire in it, they'll say that you're encouraging kids to burn things. And that would be trouble."

"That's a bunch of crap," I said.

"Yeah," said Anna, coming to my defense. "If he shows something to do with a girl getting her period, will that encourage kids to bleed?" I think I blushed a bit, but Anna didn't.

"I happen to agree with you," he said. "But they don't want to leave themselves open to getting sued. And anyway, you're really sort of toeing the line with this video to start with. It's pretty risqué."

"It's art!" I practically shouted.

"I know," he said. "That's why I'm going to approve the rest of this, at least for now, though you might have to simplify it a bit to keep the school board happy. Just no explosions."

"It was Smollet, wasn't it?" I asked. "She's the one who told you you'd get sued, right?"

"It's . . . just the rule," he said, not answering my question, which made it pretty clear that it had been Smollet, all right.

Unfortunately, things went downhill from there. In history, Coach Wilkins pulled a pop quiz on Manifest Destiny on us, and, though I knew most of the basics, I hadn't paid attention to all the key terms or vocabulary words, so I only got about a D on it.

A few seats ahead of me sat Joe Griffin, the religious creep, and midway through Coach Wilkins's follow-up lecture on Davy Crockett, he passed me a note.

It read, "Why are you wearing that shirt?"

I was wearing a T-shirt with a peace sign on it. I wrote "Why not?" on the note and sent it back up front. He probably thought that wearing a peace sign meant I took a lot of acid.

A few minutes later, it came back with "Why do you listen to heavy metal?" on it. Once again, I wrote "Why not?" and sent it back, with the note "Does God approve of passing notes?" at the bottom.

This went on for a few minutes. Over the course of the class, he asked me why I sat in the back, why I hung out with a communist, and other little stupid things. I always just answered with "Why not?" This wasn't exactly harmful or anything, but I was sure that he was just doing it to be a jerk, not because he was genuinely curious about what made me tick.

My family wasn't particularly religious, but I'd say we were as religious as anyone else I knew. Every now and then, like when somebody was sick, we'd get dressed up and go to some church or another, and we usually showed up on Easter and Christmas, but that was about it. Still, I had read the Bible from cover to cover the year before, just so I could argue with Joe about it.

Joe passed the note back.

At the bottom, he'd written, "Why are you making an obscene movie?" I wondered how he'd even heard about it.

"I'm not," I wrote back. "It's an artsy one. And an informative one." I passed it up, and it came back in a second.

"Informative about what?" he wrote.

"Sex and adolescence. In an artsy way," I replied.

It came back with his best question yet: "Aren't you encouraging people to fornicate?"

"Fornicate"! I love that word. I've never really heard anyone use it, but it actually sounds a lot dirtier than regular old sex. Playing the field is one thing, but how would you like to be known as one who fornicates?

"No," I wrote back, hoping he could see the sarcasm in my handwriting. "I'm encouraging people to masturbate. Starting with you. You need to relieve some tension."

Ha. I thought that would make a fine last word, but a few minutes later, the paper came back to me.

"God doesn't like it," he wrote back, predictably.

I had to admit that even though I disagreed with Joe on just about everything, I kind of enjoyed arguing with him. It helped kill time during a dull class, which even Coach Wilkins's imitation of Davy Crockett begging the Mexicans not to stab him to death at the Alamo couldn't save.

Lunch was a relief; at least I would be surrounded by people I liked. As soon as I sat down, Anna turned to me and said, "Did you know that in the eighteenth century in Hungary there were twelve hundred villages populated entirely by poor nobles? Like counts and dukes and stuff?"

"Twelve hundred?" I asked. "There must have been a hell of a lot of nobles to begin with."

"Maybe that's why they were all poor," said Anna. "There were so many of them that there wasn't enough money going around for all of them."

"I wish I'd been there," said Brian. "If there were a

whole bunch of poor counts roaming around, I could buy a title off one of them cheap. Then I'd be Count Brian."

"Like one of them who didn't support the very idea of nobility?" asked Edie.

"Yeah," said Brian, nodding. "Some commie count who was looking for a fast buck."

I told them all about my note-passing battle with Joe Griffin, and everyone had a good laugh. Anna said that a couple of days earlier, he'd told her whole biology class that America was doomed because kids weren't allowed to pray in school. Exactly what this had to do with biology went unexplained.

"You know," I said. "You actually are allowed to pray in school. You can pray anytime you want, the law just keeps the schools from organizing a special time for kids to do it. The only rule against doing it yourself is that you can't disrupt the class."

Anna laughed. "Damn," she said. "I was planning to spend my next math class praying to Satan at the top of my lungs." She dug into her backpack and pulled out a pair of devil horns, the kind you get in Halloween costumes, and put them on.

"I think they should have prayer in school," she said, "because then I could claim that I was a Satanist. I could demand a minute every morning to slaughter a goat, and they'd have to give it to me!"

I doubted that was true but laughed anyway.

"Did you bring those for Smollet's class?" Brian asked.

"Why else?" asked Anna.

None of us were actually Satanists. Anna and her parents went to synagogue pretty regularly, and I knew that Dustin's parents made him go to church every weekend, but Mrs. Smollet got so freaked out by us just joking about it that we couldn't help it. Sometimes I worried that it was a bit sacreligious to pretend to be a devil worshipper, but I was pretty sure that if God knew anything about what it was like to be in a class headed by Mrs. Smollet, He wouldn't mind too much. He obviously knew that we weren't actually sacrificing goats to anybody.

This brightened up my day a bit, especially since it reminded me that Halloween, the greatest holiday in the history of the world, was less than two months away, but it didn't really pull me out of the bad mood I'd been in since hearing that I couldn't do the explosion. That's the kind of thing a guy doesn't get over too quickly.

The fact that the next class was gym didn't help matters. Guys like Nick Norton always think gym is the highlight of the day, but I've never liked it much. I thought it was okay in elementary school, when all we did was play around with parachutes and stuff, until one day when we were playing elimination, which was like free-form, every-man-for-himself dodgeball, and Todd Moreland cornered me against a wall and threw a ball at my chest. I jumped straight up to get out of the way, and very nearly made it, which would have been really cool. But I didn't jump high enough, and instead of hitting my chest, the ball creamed me in the nuts. That pretty well killed my appetite for gym. And anyway, some kid a couple of towns over had had something similar happen and had to get one of his nuts removed at the hospital, or so the story went. I preferred classes where I wasn't in that sort of danger.

If teachers hadn't been watching us like hawks and ready to suspend anyone who missed a class, I would've cut gym every day. All we did was sit around in some smelly locker room, change into nasty clothes, and then run around the stupid gym while Coach Hunter shouted at us like we were in the marines or something. I swear to God that the maniac once shouted at me and called me a girl when I made a mistake during square dancing. Why the hell did we have square dancing in gym anyway?

The only guy from my lunch table I had gym with was James Cole, who was about as interested in the whole thing as I was. He was standing next to me while we were all doing the usual exercises.

"Ten push-ups!" shouted Coach Hunter. "Drop! Now!"

We all dropped, and, by going at a slower pace, I got away with doing only six or seven. Then he shouted for us all to get up and start touching our toes.

James suddenly hopped about two feet closer to me and muttered, "Bongos at twelve o'clock."

"What the hell?" I asked. "Bongos" must've been one of his newer slang inventions; I didn't know if it meant that he had muscle spasms in his back or someone had farted or what.

"Bongos!" he said, pointing his chin in front of us. I looked up and saw that Rachel Strutt was touching her toes directly in front of us, and found out right away what "bongos" were. She was wearing this loose-fitting shirt that hung down low when she bent over, and you could see right up it.

She was wearing a sports bra and all, but, well, still. It was the kind of sight that helped a guy get through the day.

A few minutes later the coach was barking for us all to run laps around the gym. As usual, James and I just walked. As we passed the coach one time, he started walking along with us.

"I'm sick of you girls," he said.

"Don't you worry that calling us girls could leave us with unresolved gender issues?" I asked. I figured that if the school was that concerned about getting sued over an explosion, they wouldn't want a teacher going around calling us girls when we certainly weren't.

"Don't smart-mouth me," he said. I think gym teachers don't like any part of you to be all that smart. "Every day I see you two girls in here giving twenty percent. I want to see some improvement."

"Twenty-one percent it is, sir!" said James, with as much conviction as he could manage. I smiled, nodded, and kept on walking. I normally make it a rule only to run if something is chasing me, and not something small. Something like a bear. And there aren't any bears in Cornersville.

So we ended up being made to run a full three laps as fast as we could, to keep from getting detention and a failing grade. By the end of it, I was a mess, sweating like a pig and probably smelling about like one, too. The five seconds or so that we got to shower afterward wasn't enough to help, and all this just a few hours before I had to go to Anna's house.

Poor James had it even worse than I did; he was panting and wheezing after the first lap, and coughing so much I was afraid his guts might come flying out. I know marijuana isn't the most harmful drug in the world, but it sure does make a guy cough.

Now, I'm not a violent person. I never really get into fights, partly because I know that, realistically, most of the guys in school could probably beat the crap out of me, and partly because I know that I just couldn't bring myself to really hurt anybody. I couldn't kick a guy in the face, even a guy I really hated. But all through the last hour or two of classes, every time some kid threw a piece of paper that ended up on my desk, I just wanted to punch the guy's lights out. I knew it wouldn't really help my problems and all that stuff that they drill into your head starting in kindergarten, but it would have at least made me feel better for a second.

In math, the last class I had before gifted pool, I came as close as I've ever come to decking someone. By that point, I was in a pretty bad mood. If there's a kid alive who's in a good mood after being barked at by a wannabe marine, I'm not sure I even want to meet that kid.

Math was occasionally fun. Not because math itself is any fun, but because Mrs. Wellington would usually just teach for about five minutes, then give us the rest of the time to do worksheets and stuff. This gave us plenty of time for screwing around, and there were days when that was a blast. That afternoon, however, I was just not in the mood.

I was about halfway through a multiplying fractions worksheet when a couple of guys I knew only from gym class came over to my desk. They both wore the sort of mini–bowl cuts soccer players tended to favor at my school.

"Are you really screwing Anna Brandenburg?" one of them asked.

"Who told you that?" I asked, getting pissed off already.

"It's like, general knowledge," said the other.

"Well, it's not true," I said.

"Why?" asked the first jerk. "Is it because you're gay?"

"Who are you gay with?" asked the second. Damn. They were teaming up on me.

Now, normally I might've said that they were probably the gay ones, but I didn't want to get into it. I just muttered, "I'm not gay. And people with pudding-bowl haircuts don't get a lot of room to make fun of anyone else!"

One of them sort of shoved my shoulder. "Yeah, well look at your hair, retard!" he said, running his hand through my hair, which was already sort of messed up.

"Hey," I said. "You think I'm the gay one? You can't keep your hands off me!"

"Go to hell," said the guy, though he stopped touching my hair. "I'll bet you *are* gay."

"Yeah, well, I'll bet you're a hermaphrodite. Go look it up."

The other guy shoved my other shoulder. "Brain," he said. I wondered why he didn't just say "Nerd." Maybe that term is out of date.

I stood up. I turned around to face them, and I got my hand into a fist. I was just about ready to use it, too; then I heard Keith Messersmith saying, "Hey, leave Leon alone. He likes metal."

"I'll just *bet* he likes metal!" said Jerk Number One. "He probably listens to boy bands."

And that was it. My fist was all set to go, and I was about the closest I had come all through middle school to punching someone. But there were two of them, and I wasn't about to get in trouble over them. So I just said, "Yeah? You probably listen to old folksingers who sing about rainbows all the time." Then I slammed my book shut and announced that I had to use the facilities.

"The gym facilities?" asked Mrs. Wellington, trying to be funny. "You can use those during gym class."

I grabbed my bag and threw my pencil against the wall with every ounce of strength I had, hoping it would shatter into a million pieces, though it just clunked against the painted cinder blocks and fell to the floor. She knew perfectly well which facilities I meant, so, figuring that it would be easier to get forgiveness later than to wait for her to quit screwing around and give me permission, I walked out of the room and headed for the boys' room. No one followed.

That wasn't the worst encounter you could have with guys who had bowl cuts and thought they were hot stuff, but I just wasn't in the mood for that kind of bullshit. If I had to listen to them rattling on like a couple of morons for five more seconds, I might've actually punched them or something. I was so mad I was practically seething as I walked along thinking about the soccer jerks and imagining how they were going to grow up. They'd probably major in financial management or something like that. Or they'd become gym teachers. I'd always wondered what kind of son of a bitch grows up wanting to be a gym teacher. That made me think about gym class and all that crap. I thought about not being able to have an explosion in the movie. Everything was bullshit—was this all the world had to offer? I imagined myself being shown the whole world by some angel, like in an old movie, and saying, "Well, I see that you've worked hard, but this sort of sucks. What else can you show me?"

The very notion of going back to class and sitting through the rest of math just seemed absurd, so I sat there on the toilet, with my pants still up, for several minutes. God, I wanted to punch those idiots.

Over on the wall next to me, which was covered in a thin layer or paint, I could still make out something Dustin had written the year before, back when he was still just doing limericks:

> There once was a kid named Dan
> Who got his butt stuck in the can
> But before you say "dumbass"
> Remember—he missed class
> (He was really a very smart man)

Amen, brother.

I stayed in the bathroom until math was a few minutes from over, making it the closest I'd ever come to skipping a class. One couldn't get away with the ol' bathroom excuse every day, and I figured I'd be lucky if Mrs. Wellington didn't catch on, but being suspended would be better than sitting through the rest of that class. And anyway, the suspension if I'd punched those guys would have been longer than the one I could get for cutting a third of a class.

I eventually got out and sneakily wandered around to

the gifted-pool room. I was five minutes early, but I still wasn't the first one there. Brian and Edie were already on the couch, making out. The gifted-pool room was supposed to be a more relaxed environment, but it still seemed about like a classroom; if I'd been in charge, I would have taken out the desks and put in some beanbag chairs. The thought of sitting in a desk again just then made me just about physically sick, so I went and joined Brian and Edie on the couch. Climbing aboard with a couple that was probably just a short jaunt from second base wasn't something I'd normally do, but these were special circumstances.

Dustin came in a few minutes later; Jenny Kurosawa, a girl from Japan who had already gotten some seriously high score on the SAT, followed him, and both of them got onto the couch, too. Then Anna came in, still wearing her devil horns, and then James and a few other various people who I hadn't really seen all summer and weren't in the advanced studies activity.

Pretty soon the couch was full, but the people coming in got the idea that the couch was the place to be, so they just piled on top of those of us who were already there, until there were about ten or twelve people stacked up on the couch. Jenny's butt was crammed into my arm, which wasn't that bad, but between that and getting such a good view of Rachel's bra in gym I was pretty sure that I wouldn't have any luck left for Anna's house.

Mrs. Smollet finally came in, carrying what looked like an armload of crossword puzzles, and made a really disgusted face at us, like she was silently horrified that we weren't acting more like kids from a sitcom set in 1956. She was one of those people who thought 1956 was America's best year. Apparently, she didn't know what awful food people used to cook back then.

Right away, she ordered us all to get off the couch and I ended up back in a desk. Some relaxed atmosphere.

"All right," she said, "did everyone have a good summer?" According to scholars, no teacher has ever come up with a more interesting greeting for a first meeting with students after the break.

We all sort of grumbled, and she began to call the roll.

"Anna Simone Brandenburg?"

"Physically here," said Anna.

"James Patrick Cole?"

James belched; Mrs. Smollet rolled her eyes.

"Dustin Michael Eddlebeck?"

"He died in a car accident," said Dustin.

She was halfway to my name before I realized that she was using people's middle names, like that would magically make us more intellectual. I started to panic.

"Leon . . . ," she began.

"Here!" I shouted, hoping she wouldn't finish. But she did.

"Leon Noside Harris, here?" she repeated. About half the class turned and looked.

"What kind of name is that?" asked Jenny. She wasn't being mean; she sounded like she was genuinely curious.

"It's, uh, some ancestor of mine. Noside Magwitch Harris, Esquire. He was a real big shot."

"That's fascinating, Leon," said Mrs. Smollet, who certainly couldn't just politely let it go. "Maybe for one of your projects this year you could research his life!"

"Well, I'm pretty busy with projects right now," I said, going for evasive action.

Her eyes narrowed. "Yes," she said. "You mean the advanced studies project?"

"Yeah. I'm doing an art film."

"Well," she said, "as I understand it, you're doing a porno film."

"No," I said, narrowing my own eyes. "It's art. And it's educational."

"Well, just so you know," she said, "I wouldn't push my luck if I were you. You know the limits."

"Sure," I said. And we stared each other down for a minute or so. "But isn't this program supposed to encourage our young minds to push the limits of what we can do? So we don't end up as stupid as everybody else in this town?"

"Just watch it, Leon," she said. "The last thing the school needs is to spend all its money on a lawsuit. It needs that money for fixing up the gym." And she went back to calling the roll.

When she finished, she gave Anna a "come on, don't give me this crap" look. "Miss Brandenburg," she said, "please remove the devil horns."

"Nope," said Anna, shaking her head. "It's no different than wearing a cross necklace."

"But what it signifies is different," said Mrs. Smollet.

"Not to a Satanist," said Anna.

"We're all Satanists," said Brian, raising his hand and making it into the devil sign. Most of us stuck out our tongues and tried to look all evil for a minute or two. Dustin, who was, at that moment, actually wearing a cross necklace, looked especially evil.

"You're not Satanists," said Mrs. Smollet, rolling her eyes.

"I know I'm not," said Edie. "Religion is the opiate of the masses."

Mrs. Smollet sighed and threw her hands up. "You guys, this is not the way to start out the year. This is the gifted pool, not the weirdo club. We're trying to do this as something fun for you. We can take it away if you want us to. I can have you all go right back to your regular classes. And if you don't get those horns off your head, Anna, I'm going to arrange for you to be sent to St. Julian's instead."

"I don't think they take my kind," she said. I don't know if she meant that they wouldn't take her because she was Jewish or if she was still pretending to be a devil worshipper, but she took the horns off. They were back on her head a minute later, though.

We all settled down for a moment; Mrs. Smollet's threats to disband the program usually shut us up for a minute.

She spent the rest of the hour telling us about all the "great" activities we were going to be doing as gifted-pool projects. Like we'd research someone from history who "meant something" to us and give a presentation on them. I decided that I'd make up a whole bunch of crap about Noside Magwitch Harris, Esquire, like maybe he was an advisor to the Queen who ended up getting executed for daring to believe in evolution or something. Yeah, that was it.

I'd say he'd been betrayed by someone named Smollet, and as he was being dragged away to have his head chopped off, he vowed that his children's children would one day have their revenge. If she called me on it, I'd accuse her of mocking my heritage, and next thing she knew she'd be serving pie down at Baker's Square for a living.

While she was yammering on, this guy named Marcus Clinch leaned across two desks and said to me, "I hear you just about got in a fight with some soccer knockers today."

"Up shut," I told him. "Don't wanna talk about it." He'd been in a class with me the year before where the teacher had a real thing about not letting anyone say "shut up," so we'd all taken to saying "up shut" instead. It still ticked her off, but she was at least smart enough to know when she was beaten. That was one of the greater victories we'd scored over teachers through the years.

"What was that, Leon?" asked Mrs. Smollet, turning around. I thought for a split second that I should say that Marcus said his ancestors could've beaten mine up, but I knew that if I did she'd give him in-school suspension and maybe make him watch a video about being more sensitive to other cultures, which I wouldn't wish on anyone, so I just said, "Nothing."

For the rest of the class, whenever Mrs. Smollet turned her back to write something on the board, everyone in the room stuck up their middle finger at her, then quickly hid their hands when she turned around. We did a lousy job of not snickering about it, but she never caught on. She herself, apparently, was not really gifted pool material.

On one level, I sort of felt bad for giving her a hard time.

But I knew that she had no intention of giving *us* an easy time, and anyway, taking my mood out on her was probably a safer way of handling it than punching a couple of soccer players.

However, for the last ten minutes of class, she gave us a lecture on family values and crap like that while we all wrote "I am not a Satanist" twenty times on notebook paper. We could, she pointed out, have been using the time to work on logic puzzles, but we just *had* to act like hooligans.

In all, I was very, very glad that it was the end of the day. It was time to go to Anna's house.

8

Anna was the first person I knew who didn't say the Pledge of Allegiance, a habit that spread pretty rapidly. Not that she made a big deal about it or anything. I just noticed one morning in seventh grade that when everyone else was putting their right hand on their heart and reciting the Pledge in homeroom, she just stood there, not saying a word. Then she gave the flag a little salute with two fingers when everyone else was saying "with liberty and justice for all."

I never asked her why she didn't say it; I guess it was simply because she didn't feel like reciting a loyalty oath to start her day. After a while, I stopped saying it myself. Not that I had anything against America; the country had my allegiance, but the more I thought about it, the more I didn't want to pledge to be loyal forever. What if the government just decided that the whole Bill of Rights business was passé and Mrs. Smollet became the president? I don't think they'd have my allegiance anymore.

Pretty soon, everyone I knew in the gifted pool was standing there and just giving a little salute during the Pledge, though none of us meant anything malicious by it—except for Edie, of course. Whenever someone tried to drill us on why we weren't saying the Pledge, she'd tell them how it was written by some socialist guy back in the eighteen hundreds. Why this didn't make her *want* to say it remained unexplained.

After the gifted-pool meeting, Anna just walked out of the room with me, and we started heading for her house, which was maybe a mile away. We got a bit stalled at the edge of the parking lot when Anna looked over at the school cop, whose job was to hang out at the edge of the parking lot, watching for any drug dealers who might be hanging around, and said, "Ooh! It's a new cop!" She ran right over to the car and peered in at the guy. I followed, wondering what she was up to.

"Hi!" said Anna. "Are you a good cop or a bad cop?"

The guy neither smiled nor frowned; he was like one of those guards in England who aren't allowed to react. "We're all good cops," he said, as if we would believe him.

"Have you caught any troublemakers yet?" Anna asked.

"Are you one?" He eyed her suspiciously.

She nodded. "Most definitely."

The cop stared at her for a second from behind his sunglasses—and so did I. I had always been told in no uncertain terms to respect police officers. But then again, she wasn't being disrespectful, she was just making conversation. Even when she said she was "most definitely" a troublemaker, he didn't pull out the handcuffs or anything.

"So," she said. "If you could slap any celebrity, who would it be?"

"We don't slap people," he said.

"She means hypothetically," I said. I wasn't about to stand around idly while she bravely interviewed the cop. She'd think I was a wimp.

"Well," he said, "that's a good question. Do I only get one slap?"

"Yes," I said, hoping that was right.

"Hmmm . . . ," he said. "Do those lawyers who advertise on TV count as celebrities?"

"Sure," said Anna. "They're on TV."

"Okay, then," said the cop. "I'd slap Gordon Griffin."

"The personal injury lawyer?" asked Anna. Joe Griffin's father. I smiled.

"Yeah. He's a jerk."

"Excellent choice," said Anna. "Have you ever met him?"

"Every cop in town has had to deal with him in court," he said. "He's an even bigger slimeball in person."

I couldn't believe that the cop had just called another adult a slimeball in front of us. I mean, was he allowed to do that?

"My dad says that he wouldn't hire that guy to stick his head down our toilet, because he doesn't want anything that gross going down there," Anna said, and I had to cover my hand with my mouth—which did not look cool—to keep from laughing so hard as to attract attention.

The cop chuckled a bit, too. "Your dad's a smart man," he said.

"His son is a jerk, too," I said. "He's always saying that

99

God disagrees with everyone he disagrees with." I hoped Joe wasn't close enough to be within earshot.

"I know the type," said the cop, who was starting to go back to looking around the campus to see if anyone was causing trouble, which, after all, was his job. "Do you guys have someplace you need to be?"

"Yes," Anna said. "We need to go buy some lighters." This was just rubbing his nose in it; he couldn't arrest us for conspiracy to buy lighters.

"You're a little young for those, aren't you?" he asked. This was all he could really say.

"I'm also too young to be appointed special environmental advisor to the mayor," she said. "But I was." I figured it wasn't true, but I wouldn't have put it past her. The girl knew her politics.

The cop stared at her for a second, probably making sure her shoes weren't covered in plastic explosives or something.

"Anyway, we'd best be on our way," Anna said. "There are young minds to corrupt."

"Well . . . okay," said the cop. "Stay out of trouble."

"No promises," said Anna. She walked away and I followed her.

"That was awesome!" I said. I was feeling better already.

"I always do that with cops," she said. "For the record, if you ask them to get you a glass of water, because they're a public servant, they don't like it very much."

I told her I didn't doubt it.

As we walked along, I felt almost inhumanly better.

Between the cop interview and the hour spent flicking Mrs. Smollet off, all the crap that was bugging me from gym, the note-passing battle, and those jerks in math class was just gone, like it had all happened a hundred years before. By the time we got to her house, I was feeling good.

On the outside, her house looked about like all the others in the area—just a normal white house. It was when you saw the inside that you realized that the people who owned the house weren't your average denizens of Cornersville. The first thing you saw was a massive framed print of a skeleton with a cigarette hanging out of its mouth. All along the hallway leading into the kitchen were more weird prints like that. Melting clocks, hairy prostitutes, and all sorts of weird stuff, all by some of the great master painters. The smoking skeleton was a Van Gogh, for example.

Anna led me into the living room, which was more of a library. There were shelves everywhere, all crammed with books. None of them looked like crappy cookbooks. I checked.

"This is the best house ever," I said. "You guys would be perfect for people playing 'What Do They Have?' "

"We're national champs three years running," she said. "Anyway, we like it."

It was the sort of house that made me want to make something of my life. I wanted to know all about the eighteenth century. I wanted art all over my walls, which, at the time, were covered mainly with posters for metal bands. Metal was cool and all, but the stuff around here was a whole different kind of cool. It was hip. It was intellectual.

It represented the kind of lifestyle that accounting school would not get me ready for.

And, just as much, I wanted Anna. I wanted to watch her read. I wanted to hear the noises her throat made when she drank a can of Coke. I wanted to feel her fingers running through my hair. I wanted to know what her teeth tasted like. But the thought of saying that out loud almost made me physically ill.

"Well," said Anna while I was looking at all the books on the shelves, "do you want to see how my movie came out?"

"Of course," I said. I sat down on the couch while she cued it up, and a large brown tabby cat jumped onto my lap.

"Why, hello," I said, stroking its ears.

"That's Spinach," she said, sitting down next to me. "He won't bite. But he likes watching TV."

My cat isn't that friendly, especially around strangers. I think he's been spooked by too many loud noises—and flooded basements—over the years.

So Spinach the cat and I stared at the screen as the movie came up. The title was *Smoking, Drugs, and Drinking: Three Ways to End Up Like a Dead Writer*. The whole movie consisted of a bunch of pictures of authors with Anna doing voice-overs.

First there was a picture of Mark Twain holding a pipe, and Anna's voice said, "Mark Twain wrote *Tom Sawyer*. He smoked like a chimney."

That was followed by a picture of F. Scott Fitzgerald, who "drank like a fish." Then came Edgar Allan Poe, who "really thought opium was keen." This went on for a while, until you became quite aware that you were spending most of your English class studying a bunch of junkies. Then there was a shot of that painting of the smoking skeleton, and Anna's voice said, "All of these people ended up dead. Some ended up dead in the gutter. Many were dirt poor when they died, even though they were famous. Still wanna take drugs?"

And that was the end.

"What do you think?" she asked.

"It was great," I said, though I wasn't sure it made me less likely to take up smoking. It didn't make it *more* likely, I guess.

Just about then, the door opened, and Anna's father walked in. He was dressed in a brown tweed coat, the kind professors on TV always wear. I guess they wear them in real life, too. Not like inventors, who probably *don't* really wear lab coats.

"Hey, Anna," he said.

"Hi, Warren," she replied. I knew she called her parents by their first names, but it still seemed weird.

"And you must be Leon," he said, holding out his hand, which I shook. "We've met before, right?"

"Just briefly," I said.

"How's the avant-garde movie coming?" he asked. I guessed Anna had told him about it.

"We were going to work on it today," said Anna. "Did you get that movie you were talking about?" Her father held up an old videocassette.

"Sure did," he said. He turned to me. "I thought you guys should see this movie."

"Is it avant-garde?" I asked.

He smiled. "Are you kidding? This one makes *La Dolce Vita* look like *Bambi*. It doesn't make any sense at all."

"Sweet," I said. "What's it called?"

"*Un Chien Andalou*," he said. "It was made by these guys back in the twenties; one of them was Salvador Dalí, the guy who painted that picture in the hallway with the melting clocks. He was really a bizarre character. You two want some coffee? I'll get some brewing."

Coffee? No one had ever offered me coffee before; most people were still offering me Kool-Aid. I had only had coffee once, after a band concert in fifth grade, during the three or four months that I played the trombone. At the reception after the concert, I'd tried to have a cup, but I accidentally got some out of a pot that had been turned off hours earlier, and the coffee in it was cold and disgusting. Still, I said, "Sure, that sounds good," not wanting to look like a wimp.

Anna and I followed him into the kitchen, where he fired up a coffee machine.

"How was school today?" he asked Anna.

"The usual bullshit," she said. I tried to play it cool again, but I'd certainly never seen anyone say "bullshit" in front of her father. I'd always sort of imagined that if you cussed in front of your parents, a SWAT team would suddenly burst in through the windows and take you off to juvenile hall. But no one showed up, and her dad didn't flinch.

"Don't worry," he said. "It'll all be over in a couple of years. If you can get through junior high, you could go off to war and be fine."

A minute later he poured three cups of coffee. "Cream and sugar?" he asked.

"Sure," I said. I was under the impression that that made it tastier, and figured I could use all the help I could get. The coffee with cream was a light tan color, and it wasn't bad. I figured I could get used to it.

We all went into the living room, and Anna's dad popped the movie into the player and turned on the TV.

Man, if you've never seen *Un Chien Andalou*, and I really doubt you have, then I'm here to tell you that it is seriously messed up. It's all black-and-white and silent, because it's so old, but I don't think putting it in color or having people talk could have possibly made it stranger.

It turns out that "un chien andalou" is French for "a dog from Andalusia," which has nothing to do with the movie. It opens with a shot of this guy sharpening his razor, like he's going to shave, and then he uses it to slice his girlfriend's eye open for no particular reason. Then he looks out the window for a long time, and spends a lot of time staring at his hands, which are covered in ants. Then, for some reason, a guy drags a grand piano, which has priests and dead donkeys on top of it, through the living room. Then, suddenly, after about fifteen minutes, it ends. Like I said, it was completely messed up. In a lot of ways, it seemed like a music video, but at least there's a point to videos—they're supposed to make you want to buy music. This seemed like it was just being weird for the sake of being weird.

Anna turned off the TV and I just sort of stared at the blank screen for a while. That seemed like the thing to do.

"That was the weirdest thing I've ever seen," I said.

"You know," said Anna's father, "when they first showed that movie, the guys who made it came with pockets full of rocks, in case the crowd rioted and they had to throw something at them."

"Really?" I asked.

"Yeah. Their idea was to make it so films and life didn't have to make sense, and things didn't have to be logical and ordered, and they thought that making weird movies would help tear down all the old rules of society and bring normal people out of their stupor. They sort of thought of themselves as activists, not just artists."

"It must have worked," said Anna. "You can put anything you want in a movie nowadays, and hardly anybody would riot." Well, I could think of a few people who would. Mrs. Smollet was probably always looking for a reason to disapprove of a movie.

"Exactly," he said. "I don't know if they made people any less stupid, but the movies must have worked."

This was just sort of an offhand comment that Anna's father made, but as far as I was concerned, it was like I was standing below a balcony, hearing a guy in a suit give a rousing speech inspiring me to take action. Suddenly, making the movie wasn't just a class project. It was a mission. I was going to be like those guys from the twenties. I was going to make a movie that would wake the sixth and seventh graders out of their stupor and change the way they thought about sex and puberty. Mrs. Smollet and the school board could just take a rock to the head if they didn't like it. And there'd be an explosion, all right. No matter what Mr. Streich said, I was going to end the movie with an explosion scene.

"Sorry about that," Anna said after her father left.

"About what?" I asked.

"Him," she said, as if I should have known. "I mean, he's okay as parents go, but sometimes he's just . . . I don't know."

"I didn't see anything wrong with him," I said.

"Well, you know. . . . He can be a bit over the top sometimes. And he could have just given us the movie and left us alone. He didn't have to watch it with us, for God's sake."

"Don't worry about it," I said. I was a bit mystified. Mr. Brandenburg was the coolest dad in the whole history of Cornersville. What did she have to be embarrassed about? He wasn't wearing a lab coat. He didn't give her the middle name Noside.

But I didn't think about it very long, because I was too busy getting ideas for the movie. This was going to be the greatest thing any sixth or seventh grader had ever seen.

9

I walked home that night with a backpack full of art. Anna and I had spent the whole rest of the late afternoon digging through all her parents' art books, marking off pictures we could put into the video. After a couple of minutes, it had even stopped being embarrassing to be looking at pictures of naked people with her, though I'll admit that I was pretty turned on the entire time. Before I left I almost felt like I should try to kiss her, the afternoon had gone so well. But I could imagine that whole scene too clearly. I'd lean in for a kiss, and she'd recoil and say, "What are you doing?" and then she wouldn't even want to talk to me for days and sitting at the same table at lunch would be too awkward to bear.

But all that aside, I had a whole stack of good pictures to use. It was looking like most of the movie could be made up of a whole bunch of still pictures, flashing in and out, with maybe some actual scenes where people moved around.

Like the kissing scene, starring Brian and Edie, which would build up to the explosion at the end.

About half of the pictures were from old paintings of naked people, most of which were pretty realistic, though some were pretty weird-looking. That was okay. Weird was good. Besides that, there were a lot of weird-looking paintings that we just thought would look interesting.

The movie didn't have to make sense; I didn't even really plan to follow the outline. To keep it educational, I'd just have a voice-over that would make sense but that, next to all the weird pictures, would actually make the movie seem even weirder.

I was starting to confuse myself. But that, too, was okay. Avant-garde art was supposed to be confusing; that was the whole point!

When I got home, my parents were already in the kitchen, cooking, to my delight, nothing more deadly than some regular grilled-cheese sandwiches.

"Hi, Leon," said my father. "How's the movie coming?"

"It's *awesome*," I said, fighting off the urge to call him Nicholas, since I knew that would just invite them to drill me on why I was calling him by his first name. I didn't really feel much like explaining to my parents that I had just decided to become a hip activist. "Except that Mr. Streich said I'm not allowed to do an explosion for it."

"Max Streich said that?" Dad asked. "He loves explosions!"

"Everyone does, except for Mrs. Smollet and the dumbass school board," I said, daring to use a word that contained the a-word in front of my parents. "They said I could get hurt."

"Well, that's probably fair," said my mother. "And watch your language."

"But it's too bad," said my father. He watched me heaving my backpack onto the kitchen table. "How did that get so heavy?" he asked.

It was no heavier than it normally was; with all the textbooks I had to carry, I was afraid I was going to end up with curvature of the spine. But I'd left all my textbooks in my locker, since I knew that I wouldn't be bothering to do any homework that wasn't for the movie.

"I just borrowed a whole bunch of books of art pictures to put into the movie. . . . Do you have any, like, science books that have weird pictures in them?"

"Well, not really," said my father. "I always thought that science books with a bunch of pictures were for sissies." I should have known. I could only imagine the results of him trying to write his own science book. The periodic table probably would have been a mess.

"But you know what we do have?" asked my mother, smiling like an idiot who had just had a glass of idiot juice. And she pointed to her shelf of cookbooks.

I hadn't thought of that before; the pictures in those books tended to make the food look even more disgusting than it actually was, which was close to impossible. Putting them next to pictures of naked people might not be terribly appealing, but if that wasn't avant-garde, I didn't know what was.

I grabbed a stack of cookbooks off of the shelf and started to flip through them; my parents both looked as though they'd waited their whole lives for this day. But I ignored them, and pretty soon I had enough bizarre pictures to pad the video nicely. After seeing *Un Chien Andalou*, I realized that it didn't really have to make much sense.

That night, I set up the camcorder in my room and started to record still shots of the pictures in the books, in no particular order. I figured I could edit them later using all the gear in the media immersion room. Taking still shots wasn't exactly challenging, so pretty soon I had about five minutes' worth of footage, about half of which was of naked paintings. Some of them were full-body images; others were close-ups on the good parts of paintings where there was enough detail. It wasn't really that bad; none of the shots of women were all that explicit. In fact, the most detailed shot of a woman was a Picasso painting called *Woman Pissing*, and it didn't look remotely realistic, but it looked hilarious after a picture of what was supposed to be some form of mixed vegetable juice but actually looked like a tall glass of barf. Like the woman in the painting had just had a glass of disgusting juice that made her whole body deformed, and now she was peeing it out. By nine o'clock, I had the basic shots in place for a pretty avant-garde picture. It was missing a few important elements, like actual scenes, not just stills, and the kiss, the explosion, and the narration, but the basics were there.

Thinking about how *Un Chien Andalou* looked a lot like a music video without music, I thought a bit more about

111

what sort of music I should have. I knew I didn't want the boring, distorted music that you hear in most of documentaries they show in school—this was going to be real music.

Later on, I called Dustin.

"You know how you always said you were going to start a band?" I asked. He was always talking about starting a band called the Ashtrays, in which he'd play keyboards. His mother had been making him take piano lessons since he was five.

"Yeah. I don't have anyone else for it yet," he said. He was also making noises that indicated that he was eating a sandwich or something. It was kind of gross.

"I know, but are you pretty good at the piano?"

"I guess so."

"Could you just sort of jam on it? Like a rocking, bluesy sort of jam, for about five minutes?"

"Sure."

I told him all about how the project was going, and how I needed a long musical sound track that would play under the whole thing, but nothing with words, because there would also be some voice-overs. Dustin immediately offered to write those, in the form of poetry. I said sure, and gave him a list of all the stuff he had to work in, like how your body changes, and how having various urges and all the stuff that went with them was normal.

"Cool," he said. "So you want me to put in stuff about how everybody beats off?"

That sort of blindsided me for a second; sure, everybody does that, but I didn't know a single person who admitted it. I sure as hell didn't want to be the first. But plenty of kids were probably really getting stressed out thinking no one else did it.

"Okay," I said. "But don't go nuts or anything."

"Very funny," he said. "Nuts."

"I didn't mean that to be a joke," I said, getting a bit flustered.

"Don't worry, man. I'll have something ready for you tomorrow."

He then asked if I could bring him all the ketchup I could get my hands on for use as blood in his movie, which was about seat belts, and I agreed. My parents still had a whole stockpile from the days when they were working through a book from the eighties called *Ketchup Is a Vegetable, Too!* I hoped I would never taste the stuff again.

When I hung up, I did a little dance around my room. Man, I hadn't just decided to become hip, I *was* hip. I was a film director. Just like the guys who made *Un Chien Andalou*. Those sixth and seventh graders in advisory classes would never know what had hit them!

No one had ever told us straight up that what was happening to us, what we were thinking, was really normal. We all sort of knew, but the fact that those pamphlets they gave out said so wasn't very reassuring. These were the sort of pamphlets that made up kids' letters, in which they would say, "I didn't mean to look, but when we took showers after gym, I noticed Jonah's penis was a little bigger than mine. Does that make him more of a man than me?"

People who thought a kid might ask that, even in an anonymous pamphlet, clearly didn't know a thing about whether we were actually normal. They were just doofuses.

113

Or is the plural for that "doofi"?

I was on a roll at that point, so I called up Anna to ask her to play cello on the sound track, then had a pretty weird experience calling Jenny Kurosawa to ask if she'd jam along on her clarinet. Her parents really gave me the third degree until I convinced them that I was calling in regards to a school project. They were known to be pretty strict; Jenny was the only person I know who was ever discouraged from reading. She had to hide her science-fiction paperbacks under her bed because her mother was known to throw books that weren't assigned by a teacher into the trash. But after some arguing, they let her on the phone, and she was more than eager to get involved in the project, provided that I never even hint to her parents what kind of movie it was.

And Brian, who had a lot of recording gear and microphones and stuff, said he could record the music and narration.

Everything was set up for the movie—all I needed was the kissing scene, which Brian and Edie were all set to do, and the explosion.

I didn't care what Mr. Streich said—one way or another, there was going to be an explosion.

This was not about getting a good grade.

This was about making a film that would wake the kids out of their stupor and tell them once and for all that all the things they were worried about were perfectly normal.

This was about art.

When I got to school the next morning, I was riding high. I bummed my way through the morning scribbling ideas into my notebook, not paying a word of attention to any of the teachers. That was nothing new.

At lunch, Dustin handed me a sheet of paper and said, "How's this for the narration?"

"You're done already?" I asked.

"It wasn't very hard," he said. "I wrote it during social studies."

I looked down at it. It was written in the form of a sonnet.

<u>La Dolce Pubert</u> Narration
by Dustin Eddlebeck

We were weirdos once, and young,
Naked against the dawning of our teen years,
with thoughts we'd never express with a tongue,

about lust, and doubts, and dreams, and fears.
But all was normal, everything, every change,
every thought that kept us up, feeling like hell,
and even though at first it felt strange,
all of the whacking was normal, as well.
Renegade pituitary glands controlled our minds
like the school system only wished it could,
but as we grew older, each of us would find
that it was totally normal, and generally good.
We stood against adulthood's door,
trying to comprehend, and hoping to score.

"That's totally bizarre," I said. "It's perfect."

"Renegade pituitary glands?" asked Anna. "That's an odd metaphor."

"It works," insisted Dustin. "Wanna hear the second one?

"Of course," I said.

He cleared his throat and began.

"Everybody lost sleep thinking of size.
Hair was growing. Our bodies were growing,
sometimes too fast, or too slowly to rise,
and it scared us to death, even though knowing
that all was quite normal, nothing was wrong
with the thoughts in our heads in the night
like the chorus and riffs of our favorite songs,
which led to the whacking——it was normal and right.
Our bodies slouched toward sweet maturity
to be fully grown, developing more with each breath

116

as one day our minds would tip toward senility
and finally pull us to the cold night of death.
Feel, while you can, the sweet kiss of your youth
that brings forth the blissful explosion of truth."

The entire table was silent for a second while we figured out what to make of the whole thing. Anna spoke first.

"Blissful explosion of truth?" she asked. "How does youth bring forth a blissful explosion of truth? That's cheesy."

"It rhymes," Dustin said defensively.

"I like how you end with a line about a kiss and then one about an explosion," I said. "I should read those two lines very slowly underneath the kissing scene and the explosion at the end. But it is sort of cheesy."

"Underlining the creation and destruction dichotomy," Anna said, nodding. "That works."

"You know you mentioned that whacking off is normal in both of those, right?" asked Brian.

Dustin snickered. "Some kids probably need to hear that as often as they can, man."

This was true. I wished I'd heard that from another kid in sixth grade—I just still wasn't entirely sure I wanted to be the one to tell the others. It was sort of a loud admission that I did it myself. But I put that out of my mind for the time being.

"That's vulgar," came a voice from behind. I turned around to see that Joe Griffin had been standing behind us, probably the entire time.

"What's vulgar about it?" I asked.

"All that talk about masturbation. It's vulgar. Plus you use the h-word."

Joe Griffin was probably the last kid in the world who thought "hell" was a serious cuss word.

"What's your point?" asked Anna. "That kids in middle school don't do it?"

"You shouldn't be telling them to do it," he said, shaking his head a little.

"What are you going to do, Joe?" I asked. "Have your dad sue me for spreading pro-whacking-off propaganda in the schools? Get Mrs. Smollet to beat me up?" She probably would.

"It's sacrilegious," said Joe.

"This isn't a Catholic school," said Anna.

I knew from previous religious arguments with Joe—which was about the only kind of conversation I ever seemed to have with him—that he thought Catholics were sacrilegious, too, for some reason, but I couldn't remember exactly why.

"You still shouldn't try to corrupt kids," he said. "It's better to be tied to a millstone in the ocean than to turn children against God."

"So I'll be going to hell for this, then?" I asked. "You get to decide that?"

He shook his head. "God does," he said.

"Hell is only for those who believe in it," said Edie.

"Well," said Joe, "I believe in it."

Oh, man, I thought, just hoping no one would beat me to the joke. Verily, God had delivered him unto my hands.

"Well then, off you go!" I said. "I hope you'll send us a postcard."

Everyone laughed, and Brian gave me a high five.

Joe walked away at that point, apparently unable to think of a good comeback for that one. In a way, I almost felt sorry for the guy. His heart was in the right place—you could say that he just didn't want us to go to hell and was concerned. In reality, though, it always seemed more like he just thought he was going to heaven and assumed that we weren't, and wanted to rub that in our faces. I wondered how he'd react if he got to heaven and found all of us already there? Maybe he'd apply to move to Valhalla.

"Anyway," I said, getting back on topic, "those are perfect." I dug into my backpack and retrieved four plastic bottles of ketchup, which I gave to Dustin, per our agreement.

"I have an idea for something else we could do, a new scene," said Anna, after he was safely gone. "And I'll bet we could get out of sixth period to do it."

"Then I'm game for anything!" I said. I didn't care if what we were doing was filming ourselves scrubbing the floor with a toothbrush and singing show tunes, if it got me out of sixth period.

So we left lunch early to go to the office, where we explained that we needed permission to leave sixth period for work on a project for the advanced studies class, and got permission right away, as we usually could. You could almost always get permission to get out of a class if you mentioned something to do with the gifted pool. I think they were afraid that if they said no, we'd use our gifted intellects against them or something. And they were right.

119

Anna and I met back at the office before sixth period and signed out to do "advanced studies work."

"You still haven't told me what we're doing," I said as we walked out of the office.

"Well, first of all, we're going to check out a camera from the media immersion room," Anna said.

"What about after that?"

"You'll see!"

We checked out the camera in her name; then I followed her down the hall toward the gym, and we walked up to Coach Hunter, whose powers were useless against us, since we weren't there for gym class.

"We'd like to borrow the CPR dummy," she said. "It's for activity period." She showed him the pass the office had given us.

Old Coach Hunter rolled his eyes a bit; he tended to do that whenever he was confronted with a school issue that didn't involve throwing balls or doing push-ups. But he led us to a little utility closet and dug around until he found the dummy.

The CPR dummy was a mannequin with no legs that we had used the year before, when we'd all had to take a day-long CPR course. We used it for practicing mouth-to-mouth resuscitation, which could hardly have been very sanitary; if one person in the class had had mono, all of us would have gotten it. It seemed to me that a course in something like CPR should be, well, safe, but the whole class had an air of irrationality about it. The people who taught it were always asking us weird worst-case-scenario questions, like "What do you do if you walk into the garage and find that someone has swallowed a bottle of acid, and, in the confusion that followed, cut off one of their arms with a chain saw?"

I really should have paid attention, because, knowing my dad, the idea that that sort of thing might actually happen wasn't out of the question. But I replied, "Steal their wallet, because they're probably already dead, and try to get a head start on the cleanup." I ended up failing that course.

Anna grabbed the dummy from Coach Hunter and thanked him; then we walked off to the room where the gifted pool met. Mrs. Smollet was sitting there, doing paperwork and eating something out of a little cardboard carton.

"Hi, Mrs. Smollet!" Anna greeted her, using all the phony cheer she could muster.

"Oh, hello!" she said, looking surprised to see us. "Can I help you?"

"We're just doing some work for the movie," I said.

"Oh," she said. "Is that why you need a naked dummy?"

She really said that. I'm not making that up.

"Well," I said, "they don't really make CPR dummies that wear clothes."

"I could take off mine and loan it to the dummy," Anna offered. I was sure she didn't mean it and had just said it to see the look of horror on Mrs. Smollet's face. She couldn't have been disappointed; Mrs. Smollet looked like she was about to have a coronary.

"Well, you're not doing anything . . . untoward . . . with it, are you?" she asked. "Because I can't let you do anything obscene."

"Well," said Anna, "okay, but we might just have to edit some things out, because this dummy has a really dirty mind."

"Yeah," I said. "The poor girl has been choking to death so long she's forgotten about the power of positive thinking."

Mrs. Smollet sighed. "Okay. Just be careful," she said, and she went back to her paperwork and food.

Anna laid the dummy faceup on the couch, arranging the arms as well as she could.

"Okay," she said. "Now we just have to make it look weird. Help me out."

We spent the next few minutes digging around the room looking for stuff to put around the dummy. In the end, the dummy had a marker sticking out of its mouth, a pencil stuck in each ear, and a sign on its chest that read U R NORMAL. Then I got the idea that we could take a few shots of it, with a different sign each time. So, by the time we were done, we'd filmed the CPR dummy holding signs that said U R NORMAL, USE A CONDOM, I GROW HAIR, and I AM A DOG FROM ANDALUSIA. None of them really made much sense, except for the one about the condom, which was good advice, but all of them were fairly avant-garde.

The whole time, Mrs. Smollet sat there doing paperwork, though she couldn't resist turning to stare at us now and then. She never said anything; she was looking at us like we were plotting some sort of raid on the school.

And we were. In a way.

11

The next morning I was in the media immersion room fifteen minutes before the bell, using the editing machine to splice everything together into a rough draft of the movie—though it wouldn't have music or the narration. Just a rough cut of the shots I had. Like a demo version. I kept working all through activity period, and fifteen minutes before the bell rang, I had a cut ready to show to the class—it would just need sound, the kiss scene, and the explosion before anyone outside the class could see it. The kiss/explosion thing would make or break the whole movie, honestly. It had to go out with a bang.

It was only when I got up to tell Mr. Streich I was ready to show the movie to the class that I noticed that Mrs. Smollet had been sitting in the room the entire time.

"Finishing up, Leon?" she asked, trying to seem friendly and doing a lousy job of it.

"It's a rough cut," I explained. "It still needs a couple of important shots, but I'm going to show this version to the class today."

"Mind if I watch it with you?" she asked, as though I had a choice.

"I can't stop you," I said. Mrs. Smollet had a weird sort of position. Since she was just a program director, not a regular teacher, she really didn't have as much power as most of the people in the school. But what power she did have followed her everywhere she went, unlike some teachers, whose power was greatly diminished outside of their classrooms. Mrs. Smollet's even stretched to the high school, where she ran a couple of other programs.

Mr. Streich wheeled a TV to the front of the room, and everybody gathered around to see how my movie looked. Despite the fact that I knew I was going to have a lot of explaining to do to Mrs. Smollet, possibly including the very facts of life, I had rarely been more excited in my life. I was a filmmaker!

The movie started with just a few seconds of the words "La Dolce Pubert" on a plain screen, and I started to read the narration aloud. Then the first shot of naked artwork came in. There were a few paintings in a row, followed by a shot or two of bad-looking food, one shot of the dummy, then some footage I'd shot the night before of boiling water, which represented hormones that were about to go out of control. I was surprised by just how much it still really needed the music and the kissing and explosion scenes; those would tie it all together.

Everyone thought it looked pretty cool, though, whether it was tied together or not.

"Right on!" said Brian. "I wish they'd shown that to me when I was in sixth grade!"

"It's not really done yet," I said, for the second or third time. "It still needs those two last scenes, and then I'll probably change a bit more when I edit it again. Then there's the music."

"Still," said Edie, "it looks great the way it is! I can't wait to film my scene!" She grinned at Brian like a cat in heat.

Even Mr. Streich was about to say something nice when he was interrupted by Mrs. Smollet, who had been taking notes the entire time, only occasionally looking up at the screen.

"I'm going to need a copy of that," she said. She didn't seem happy. Then again, unless she was making some kid dress up like a famous composer or something as part of a project, she never seemed all that happy.

"What for?" I asked. She started to fumble around a bit.

"I'll need to submit a copy of it to the school board before they can show it to the younger kids," she said. "That's all. It's just a formality. And I'll need a copy of the text you're using for the narration."

It was clear from her tone that that certainly wasn't all, but I had no choice but to give her the tape.

"I'm not sure I know about that policy," said Mr. Streich. "Are you sure that's standard?"

"With sex ed it is," said Mrs. Smollet. "The board reviews every sex-ed film before it gets shown to make sure there's nothing that'll get us sued."

"I'll need it back tonight, if that's possible," I said as politely as I could manage.

125

"We'll see," she said.

I took the narration over to the copy machine and ran off a duplicate for her.

As she walked out of the room with the tape and the text, I ran over to the editing board to grab the master tape. I didn't know what the hell Mrs. Smollet really wanted a copy for—maybe it turned her on or something to see all the paintings of naked guys—but I was certainly glad that all she had was a copy. If I never got that one back, I could make another from the master in no time.

The whole thing about having to have the video reviewed by the school board didn't please me much, though the image of all of them sitting around eating popcorn and watching every sex-ed movie under the sun to decide what was appropriate and what wasn't sort of amused me. I'd hoped they'd just have an assembly where they'd pop the student-made movies in, one after the other, and I'd take them by surprise. If I had to be approved by a board, I knew that I might not make it. If I didn't, would that affect my grade?

It didn't matter. I'd manage to show it to the kids somehow.

Two hours later, while I was in history class, one of the kids who worked in the office came in and handed Coach Wilkins a note, who handed it to me.

I was to report to the office immediately. It seemed I was being suspended.

Getting suspended in middle school is not the sort of disaster than can genuinely ruin your life. A lot of kids worry that getting suspended will go on their permanent record, but that's a bunch of crap. Even by the end of elementary school, I knew that there wasn't really any such thing as a permanent record, and further knew that no prospective employer or college was going to call up the school asking for a copy of my record and then decide to reject my application because I once got in trouble in eighth grade. I mean, really! How would that work? If there was some great folder of everything I had ever done in school, which I could never access or see, why would some McDonald's manager be able to get a copy on demand? It's all just silly, if you think about it. I suppose they probably keep a record of your grades, address, and all that in their filing cabinet, in case you get famous and people in the future need proof that you went to school, but that's all.

That, however, did not mean I wanted to be suspended. As I took that long walk to the office, I felt for a second like a condemned criminal, which I was starting to feel like more and more often, but then I shook that off and made myself feel as though I was an alleged felon walking into the courtroom to argue my case. I wasn't going to go down without a fight—whatever I was fighting over. As I reached the office door, I realized that I wasn't exactly sure which offense they were suspending me for in the first place. Was it illegal to use a CPR doll for something other than its intended purpose? Had they found out that I'd spent the last third of math class in the bathroom on Tuesday? That was probably it.

When I walked into the office, the principal, Dr. Brown, was sitting at his desk, and Mrs. Smollet, surprise surprise, was sitting next to him.

"Ah, Mr. Harris," said Dr. Brown, "nice of you to join us." Dr. Brown was a friendly sort of guy, but none of us really liked him much because we could always tell that he just didn't take us that seriously. After all, he didn't give us enough credit to know that we could tell he was wearing the worst hairpiece in town.

"What am I in for?" I asked, sitting down on the other side of his desk.

"Well," he said, "we have a little complaint from Mrs. Smollet here."

"Oh?" I asked. "Do tell." I was trying my best to act all casual. Had I been braver, I would have said, "Why should today be any different?" But seeing as how I was nervous, I wasn't in the kind of mental shape you need to be in to come up with anything brilliant on the spot.

Sitting on a chair much nicer than the one I got, she was looking very stern, like one of those old paintings of Puritan women. She would have made a good Puritan; she and Joe Griffin would probably think that burning witches was fun and educational for the whole family.

"Well," said Dr. Brown, "it's all to do with your video project for advanced studies. She tells me that she warned you not to do anything inappropriate with it."

"That's right," I said. "And I didn't."

"Well, that's where we sort of disagree," he said. "I think you've done a very good job on the movie, but it's clearly inappropriate for a middle school project."

"It's not inappropriate!" I said. "It's art! Most of the suggestive images come from some of the greatest paintings ever produced."

"Well, her problem isn't really with the nudity," he said.

"Actually," Mrs. Smollet interrupted, "I do have a problem with the nudity. And with this thing you intend to use as narration. This . . . film"—she acted like saying the word "film" was physically painful to her—"is simply vulgar."

"There isn't any real nudity!" I said. "The only naked things in it are paintings and a CPR dummy."

"That doesn't matter," she said. "Nudity is nudity."

"But great paintings aren't obscene!" I said. "They're works of art."

"It's still not appropriate," she said. "If I were a mother, I wouldn't want my children to see this sort of thing."

"Well, there are points that can be made on both sides," said Dr. Brown, breaking up the argument and trying to be my pal. "But the real problem is with the, uh . . . the masturbation references. There are several in the text."

"That's right," said Mrs. Smollet. "This film goes out of its way to promote masturbation."

"It doesn't promote it, exactly," I said.

"We got a complaint about it already," she said. "One student came to me and told me that you described it as 'pro-whacking-off propaganda' and that you'd personally told him that you were using it to encourage students to masturbate. I have it in your handwriting, in fact." He held up the note he and I had passed back and forth.

Somewhere, Joe Griffin was sitting with that obnoxious smirk of his on his face, knowing that this was happening. I would have decided then and there to kick his ass, but if I gave him a personal injury, his dad would probably sue me. I guess nothing says "protection" like having your dad advertise on TV that he sues people over minor injuries.

"I was joking around!" I said.

"I think it's obviously promoting the . . . practice," she continued. "The scenes of the dummy doing it are absolutely inappropriate."

"What?" I asked. "The dummy isn't doing anything! It doesn't even have a crotch!" This was true—it was a waist-up dummy. The people who built it probably figured that legs were rarely involved in mouth-to-mouth resuscitation.

"Well, let's take a look," said Dr. Brown. He got up from his desk and walked across the room to the TV that was set up in the corner and put my tape in the machine. He fast-forwarded to a shot of the dummy that showed it only from about the chest down.

"See?" she said. "It's clearly . . . well, you know. . . ."

I looked closely. The dummy's hand was indeed right about where the crotch would have been, but it wasn't moving around or anything.

"It's not, either!" I said. "It just happens to have its hand where its crotch ought to be. What's the big deal?"

"The big deal is that this film promotes masturbation," said Mrs. Smollet.

"No, it doesn't!" I argued. "It just says that it's normal, which it is. Dummies don't usually do it, of course, which is why the dummy in the movie isn't, but it's pretty normal for people."

"Well, be that as it may," said Dr. Brown, "it's not an appropriate topic for this grade level. And please try to keep the sarcasm down so we can have an open dialogue here."

"I don't see why it's not an appropriate topic," I said.

"It's *never* an appropriate topic," said Mrs. Smollet. "Morals are morals, and this movie is simply immoral."

"That's absurd!" I said. "How is middle school an in-appropriate time to talk about that subject? If anything, it's the most appropriate time of all! You know how many kids are probably stressed out about that?"

I sort of wondered what exactly she found immoral about masturbation in the first place. Who did it harm? I'd seen the thing in the Bible about spilling one's seed instead of using it to get someone pregnant, but that surely didn't mean that eighth graders in this day and age should be going around getting people pregnant. Maybe back in bibli-cal times it was okay, but not now.

"Still," said Dr. Brown. "It's not the sort of thing that we're allowed to discuss in schools. Parents will complain. I could lose my job."

"Parents like her?" I said, pointing to Mrs. Smollet. "They probably don't want sex ed in the schools to begin with."

"Well, if you ask me," she said, stepping onto the soap-box I'd set out for her, "it's just providing a how-to manual. But that's not the point here."

I made no secret of the fact that I was rolling my eyes. "You're in charge of the gifted pool," I said. "Do you hon-estly think kids don't already know the basics?"

"Well, there's a lot of merit in your argument, Mr. Harris," said Dr. Brown, trying to shut us both up. "But the fact remains that I can't allow this sort of thing in the school, and since you were warned not to do anything that could be seen as inappropriate, we have no choice but to take action."

"Well, there's not a lot I can do that would be appropriate to Mrs. Smollet!" I said. "She'd probably be upset if I showed someone's bare ankles!"

"That's enough, Leon," she said. She looked as though she was ready to start breathing fire at any moment.

I was convinced that whoever had put her in charge of the gifted pool must have been smoking the pot that was growing in the woods behind the school. And I was further convinced that she herself must have been eating Drug Krispies for breakfast to think that something everybody did, and that was totally harmless, was such a terrible thing to talk about.

Dr. Brown was starting to drop the friendly routine. "Since this is really the first time you've been in serious trouble, we're just going to give you in-school suspension for tomorrow and for the rest of today," he said. "And don't worry; it won't go on your permanent record."

As I have said, Dr. Brown really did not take us seriously.

"Does this mean that the movie won't get shown to the sixth and seventh graders?" I asked.

"Well, of course it does," he said. "Be reasonable, Mr. Harris." Mrs. Smollet gave me a look that probably would have killed anyone under the age of twelve.

"I am," I said. "I'm the only one in here being reasonable."

"You already have a day and a half, Mr. Harris," said

Dr. Brown. "Mrs. Smollet suggested much longer. Would you like me to add more time?"

I sighed. "No," I said. "I'll go quietly. But every kid in the school is going to hear about this."

"I don't doubt that they will," said Dr. Brown.

He had no idea.

I'd never been suspended before. I'd had my fair share of detentions over the years, but those were no big deal. Show me a kid who can get through middle school without getting detention once or twice and I'll show you a kid without enough self-esteem to speak his mind.

Suspension was a whole other matter, though. People would notice I wasn't in school, and they'd talk. I fully expected that by the end of the day, Anna, Brian, Edie, Dustin, James, and everyone else would know that I was suspended, and they'd probably know exactly why, too. News travels. And no one would hesitate to guess that Mrs. Smollet was behind it.

To serve my term, I was led into a small room near the teachers' lounge that was empty except for a small table with four chairs. Dr. Brown told me to have a seat; then he walked out, shutting the door behind him. There were no bars, but I was officially in prison, and to top it off, in solitary confinement. According to my watch, I would be there for four hours that day and six and a half the next.

I don't know if the room was made just for in-school suspension, but I couldn't imagine what other purpose it served. The walls were covered with stupid motivational posters, the kind where they have a picture of an eagle or the Grand Canyon, then something like MAKE THE RIGHT CHOICE—CHOOSE SUCCESS under it. I was quite familiar with them; the previous year, my dad had decided that my schoolwork might improve if he put a bunch of them up in the bathroom, but I'd taken them down myself. The last thing I want to see when I'm in the bathroom is a sign that says COMMIT YOURSELF TO QUALITY IN ALL YOU DO. Having to spend a full day and a half surrounded by them seemed worse than spending a day in an actual prison cell.

It was a good thing I had my backpack with me, since it was just about time for lunch. I wondered what would have happened if I hadn't packed it but had planned to get the school lunch. Would they have expected me to starve? Probably not; that would be a lawsuit waiting to happen. They'd probably have had it brought in for me by some office aide. I'd compliment them on their fine catering service.

Outside, I imagined Dr. Brown was probably calling my parents, if Mrs. Smollet hadn't fought him for the honor. Mom and Dad had never found out about the times I'd been in detention, so this would be a new one for them. Their little Leon, the criminal. No, that wasn't what I was. I was no criminal. I was a supposed pornographer.

No, that still wasn't good enough. An alleged smut peddler.

Smut peddler. That was what Dr. Brown was probably telling my parents. If Smollet was there, she was probably saying I was a no-good, dirty-minded teenage hoodlum who lacked moral fiber and needed his mouth washed out with soap.

I pulled my lunch out of my backpack and ate it, just tossing the empty plastic bags and wrappers on the floor. Screw 'em. I would serve my time, but they couldn't make me be neat.

A lot of people in history, like Gandhi and some of the founding fathers and guys like that, thought it was honorable to serve time in jail for a noble cause. That was what I was doing. I was serving time for a noble cause: the right to make a frank, honest, and artistic sex-ed video. The right to tell kids that what they were going through and doing was completely normal, and that they didn't need to worry. If that wasn't a noble cause, I didn't know what was. A generation of kids who knew *that* in sixth grade could change the world for the better.

About an hour and a half went by very, very slowly. I was just starting to think that this was going to be a seriously long couple of days when the door opened, and in walked a thirty-something-year-old jerk with curly blond hair and glasses with Coke-bottle lenses. I could tell just by looking at him that he was a jerk. He was, after all, probably working for the school. That was a solid indication of jerkhood right there.

"Hi there, young man," he said. I generally do not trust guys who call me "young man."

"What's up?" I asked.

"My name is Dr. Guff," he said. "I'm the school psychiatrist." He gave me a little "I'm here to be your buddy" smile.

My ears perked up. Pay dirt! The rumors were true—he did exist! I wished I had a camera. Despite James's and Dustin's stories about meeting him, I had begun to think he really was just a legend.

"I'm Leon," I said, offering my hand. "Can I do the inkblot test?"

He laughed politely. "We don't really do that, now that everyone knows about it ahead of time," he said. "They just have me come in and rap with the kids who, you know, fall into some issues."

People who say "young man" usually say "rap" instead of "talk." It's a good way to tell when someone's trying to get you to think he's cool when he's actually, as I suspected, a jerk. If he had been taking me seriously, he would have said "they have me talk to the kids who get in trouble to make sure they aren't planning on killing anyone or anything." Actually, I think school psychiatrists are the only people left who still say "rap" when they mean "talk."

"Well," I said, "I've fallen into some issues, all right. I'm a martyr for the cause. Like that guy in the Goya painting who's being shot by the firing squad." I'd seen that picture in one of the art books I borrowed from Anna. I raised my arms, imitating him.

"Okay, good," he said, nodding. "So you feel that you're a victim in this case?"

"Sure," I said. "I didn't do anything wrong. My video is informative and artsy. This is censorship."

"Well, I guess we can call it that, if that's what you're comfortable with," he said.

"What else could it be?"

"Legally speaking," he said, "it's not censorship. The school is allowed to determine what's acceptable and what's not in this sort of case."

"Still," I said, "this is crazy. Have you seen the movie I'm in trouble over?"

"Yes"—he nodded—"and I thought it was very creative. You're a very creative student, Leon."

Say it, jerk. I thought. *Say the part about the potential.*

"You have so much potential," he said.

Yes!

"I've heard," I said. "People tell me that about every other day."

"Well," he said, "have you ever thought of applying your creativity to your schoolwork?"

"I did," I pointed out. "This movie was schoolwork. And I ended up suspended for it."

"Maybe what I'm saying," explained Dr. Guff, still using that annoying, gentle cool-guy tone, "is that you should think about finding more appropriate channels for your creativity. It's like in *Star Wars*. Luke has the Force, and he can use it for good or evil. Your creativity is like the Force. You determine your own destiny. Right now, you're using it to make inappropriate school projects."

"I've said this before," I said, "and I'm sure I'll be saying it again. There was nothing inappropriate about that movie. Saying that you can't talk about masturbation in middle school is like saying . . ." I paused to think of a good comparison. "It's like saying you can't talk about sand in the desert. Or trees in the forest."

If any psychiatrist believed that twelve-year-olds didn't think about sex, then that psychiatrist sucked at his or her job.

"That may be so," said Dr. Guff, "but it's not my call to make."

Aha! He was pulling evasive action! Washing his hands of the whole affair so I couldn't complain to him.

"Well," I said, "maybe, as school psychiatrist, you could explain the facts to them. I don't think it's ever occurred to Mrs. Smollet that anyone here ever thinks about sex."

"Let's talk about how all this makes you feel," he said, changing the subject, pulling further evasive action. "Do you ever feel angry?"

"Actually, I feel crazy," I said. "Do you know that just the other night I made a casserole out of applesauce and green beans?"

He chuckled. "Did you, now?"

"Sure did. And I ate it, too."

"So you think that makes you crazy?"

"If you can think of a better word for it, I'd like to hear it," I said. "I'm crazy, Dr. Guff. I'm crazy as a daisy. And now I'm an alleged smut peddler."

"Mm-hmm," he said, writing something in his notebook.

"And I'd like you to tell Dr. Brown and Mrs. Smollet that this isn't over. I can promise you that we won't do anything violent. We won't go on a rampage or anything, but this fight isn't over. People will hear about this. And they won't sit still for it. Can you deliver a message to Mrs. Smollet for me?"

"All right," he said.

"Here it is," I said. "Don't mess with the weirdos in the gifted pool."

He scribbled that down. "You do realize," he said, "that she requested that you be removed from the gifted pool?"

That was interesting news. I guess I shouldn't have been surprised, but I felt like he'd just kicked a stool out from under me. I wondered if she was allowed to throw me out. I hoped not. The thought of having to go to sixth period every day, every week, was almost too much. I told myself that if she could, she would have thrown most of us out a long time before.

"Well," I said, trying to stay calm, "maybe she should be removed as the gifted-pool director. And that's my final comment."

After that, as far as I was concerned, the interview was over. I sat back, folded my arms across my chest, and nodded, figuring he'd nod back, gather up his notes, and take off.

But Dr. Guff didn't quite get the message. He went right on asking insipid questions. So I decided to just have fun with him.

"Do you ever feel angry when you're at home?" he asked.

"Sure," I said. "You would, too, if you were eating apple-sauce and green bean casserole instead of just ordering a pizza."

"How about violent?" he asked. "Do you ever feel that violence is a good way to deal with your anger?"

"Well, of course I do!" I said. "Just last week I shoved my grandmother down the stairs and then jumped on her ankles over and over."

"Did you really do that, Leon?"

"Sure I did. You would, too, if you heard all the great noises old people make when you jump on them."

He just nodded and kept scribbling. I hoped he was smart enough not to take that seriously, but I wasn't certain. If he did any investigating, he'd certainly find out that my grandmothers both lived in Florida and hadn't been anywhere near my staircase lately.

"What sort of music do you like, Leon?" He acted like he was just trying to talk about something I'd be interested in, but I knew he was seeing if I listened to music that might drive me to violence.

"Metal," I said. "Heavy metal." I caught him trying not to smile, and knew that that was just what he wanted to hear.

"Why's that?" he asked. "You dig the rhythm, the beat, the tune?"

"Mostly the lyrics," I said, knowing that I was supposed to say I didn't care about the lyrics, I just liked the sound, which would have made me seem less disturbed. "They give me lots of good ideas."

"Like what?"

"Like there's this one song, by, uh . . . Supernatural Anarchy," I said, making up a band on the spot. "It's called 'Push Your Grandma Down the Stairs.' "

"I don't think I've heard of that band," he said. "Are they new?"

"Nah," I said. "They've been around for years. Their last album was called *Satan Kicks Butt*."

"Tell me about your parents, Leon," he said. I just decided to tell the truth.

"Well," I said, "my dad is an accountant, and he's really angry all the time."

"Why is he angry?" Dr. Guff asked. "Does he drink?"

"Not really," I said. "He gets angry at Thomas Edison."

"Is that a neighbor of yours?"

"No! Thomas Edison. The dead lightbulb guy." I suppose I shouldn't have thought Dr. Guff would assume I meant *that* Thomas Edison. It wasn't like it made any sense.

"The inventor? Why would he be mad at him?"

"For being a scumbag," I replied. "If Dad heard you calling Edison an inventor, he'd go ballistic."

"Uh . . . huh," said Dr. Guff. "Leon, is there a word of truth to any of the things you're telling me?"

"Actually, yes," I said. "All the stuff about the casserole is true. So is the stuff about Thomas Edison. I told you, Dr. Guff. I'm crazy. But if you want someone who really needs counseling, go talk to Mrs. Smollet. She's an absolute nut."

"I can see you have a lot of anger toward her," he said.

"Wouldn't you?" I asked.

He sat there and stared at me for a long time.

"Leon," he said, "I don't think you're crazy. I think you're a very smart, talented young man. But you need to control your emotions and keep yourself in line. This sort of thing is only going to get you in more trouble in high school."

"All right, Dr. Guff," I said. "I'll be good."

Five minutes later he was out the door. That was his whole message—try to be good and use your potential. I could have done his job without a day of training. It seemed like an easy career path, except that I think you'd have to give up a sizable chunk of your soul to take a job like that.

I wondered if he'd say the same thing to Brian, the mechanical pyro. If Brian used his potential to the fullest, he could probably build a nuclear reactor in his garage.

On the other hand, maybe Dr. Guff was wrong. Maybe I was a bit crazy. Scientifically, I certainly had genetics working against me, what with my parents and all. But the guys who made *Un Chien Andalou* had been out of their minds, so I'd at least be in good company.

Toward the end of the day, Coach Wilkins showed up in the room, with a coffee cup in his hand.

"Hi, Leon," he said, smiling and flashing me a peace sign. It was a pretty lame thing to do, but I took it as a sign that he was on my side.

"Hi, Coach Wilkins," I said.

"I understand that you're a political prisoner," he said, smiling like the whole thing was somehow funny.

"Something like that," I said. "I'm being censored."

"Well," he said, "I just wanted to sneak in here and let you know that we watched your tape in the teachers' lounge, and more than a couple of the teachers are on your side here. The whole thing reminds me of when I was in school."

"Really?" I asked.

"Sure. We were your age once, you know. When I was in college, I was part of a free-speech group called Freedom Under Charles Kerr. Think about the initials."

"That's pretty clever," I said. I was sort of surprised that he felt like he could tell me something like that without worrying about getting fired. I was going to ask who Charles Kerr was, but the day was almost over, and I knew that if I really got Wilkins started on something, I might never be able to leave. I could always find out for myself.

"Anyway, just hang in there," he said. "A lot of great art is censored when it first comes out, and that almost never stops it from being a hit. When I was in school, they tried to ban *Forever* by Judy Blume at my school, and I think every kid in town ended up reading it. They probably never would have touched it if the school board hadn't made such a big thing about it. And anyway, it's not like this will go on your permanent record or anything. So keep your chin up!"

I hate middle school. Even the teachers who are on your side don't take you that seriously. Keep my chin up?

"And Leon?" he said as he walked out the door. I turned my head to him. "Don't be surprised if everyone in school knows about this by the time classes end. I'm doing my part."

The day dragged on for what seemed like years before the bell finally rang. On my way out, Dr. Brown told me I was to report right back to the office the next day, and I said I would. If it was honorable to serve time for a noble cause, then I would serve my time.

I wanted to hang around outside the school afterward, to see what everyone had heard, but Dr. Brown insisted on escorting me out of the building and walking with me until I was off school property. I didn't say a word to him the whole time; we just slowly walked away from the building until we got to this little drainage ditch that ran under the street, which was known as the Pee Tunnel because, well, younger kids on their way back from grade school often peed in it. The tunnel marked the official edge of school property. When we got there, Dr. Brown said, "I'll see you in the morning, same time, same channel," which I guess was supposed to be funny, then turned and left me there. I just kept walking home. When I got there, my parents were waiting in the living room.

"Well, Leon," said my mother, "we got the call. I told you this would happen."

"But," said my father, "we want to make sure that we hear your side of what happened."

"Well," I said, "Mrs. Smollet saw my movie, thought it was horribly inappropriate for kids to be told that, uh"—I wasn't about to talk about masturbation in front of my parents, so I went for a nicer way of putting things—"that thinking about sex is normal."

"Well, your movie isn't explicit, is it?" asked my dad. "It wouldn't be rated R or anything, right?"

"Who knows?" I said. "You never know what they're going to decide about movies. But all the nudity in mine is just old paintings and a CPR dummy that doesn't even have a crotch."

"She told me about the dummy," said my father, half frowning. "But she didn't tell me that it didn't have a crotch."

"Mrs. Smollet called you?" I asked.

"Yes, she did," he said.

"Don't listen to her. She thinks she's the morality police."

To my great surprise, Dad chuckled. "Don't worry about me, Leon," he said. "I told you how I used to do lighting for my roommate's avant-garde stuff, right?" I nodded. "Well, there were plenty of people like her who used to show up to complain. I know how to deal with that sort of people. Of course, his show had actual nudity in it."

"Really?"

"Yeah. He used to go onstage naked and painted green every now and then. Some people in town thought that was absolutely unacceptable."

"It was, if you ask me," said my mother.

"But this is different!" I said. "My movie really has a point!"

"I'm sure it does," said my father. "I'll tell you what: I'll go into the school in the morning and talk to Dr. Brown to see if we can work something out."

I couldn't believe what I was hearing. I was in the most trouble I'd ever been in, and my dad was offering to help bail me out.

For once in my life, I was awfully glad that I'd never actually pushed anyone in my family down the stairs.

"What does Max Streich think of all this?" Dad asked.

"I'm not sure," I said. "I didn't get to talk to him yet."

"Well, I'm sure he'll be ready to fight for you," he said. "I'll give him a call later on. You'll probably have to serve out the day tomorrow regardless, but I think we can keep all this off your permanent record, at least."

About five minutes later, Anna called. "Is it true?" she asked.

"That depends," I said. "What are people saying?"

"That Mrs. Smollet suspended you over the movie."

"Yep," I said. "A day and a half in-school for being an alleged smut peddler. She thought the dummy was jerking off."

"What the green hell?" Anna asked. "Why would she think that? The dummy doesn't even have anything *to* jerk off!"

"I know!" I said. "And they aren't going to show the movie to the kids, and I'm not allowed to talk to anyone tomorrow." I was sure Dr. Brown would escort me on and off the premises again.

"This isn't over," she said. "We can finish this movie. All you need is the kissing scene, right?"

"Yeah," I said. "And the explosion and the audio. We can still tape Edie and Brian doing the kissing scene any time. And I kept the master tape." Mrs. Smollet probably didn't know this; she probably thought that the rough cut she had *was* the master tape. As I have mentioned, she wasn't that gifted herself.

"Right," Anna said. "Don't worry, we've all got your back. Let's meet up at Fat Johnny's tomorrow night and we'll figure out what we're doing. They don't know how many people are involved in this thing, do they?"

"Nope," I said. "Mrs. Smollet knows you helped, I guess,

but she doesn't know anything about Dustin or Brian or Edie being involved. But be warned—I know she wants to kick me out of the gifted pool."

"How do you know?"

"Dr. Guff told me."

"You got to talk to him?" She sounded terribly jealous.

I told her the whole story—on any other day, that would have been the first thing I'd told everyone. But this day was different—our spots in the gifted pool were at stake. Art was at stake. Freedom itself was at stake, if you got right down to it.

"Well, do you think she can kick us out?" I asked, when I was done with the story about Dr. Guff.

"I don't think so," she said. "Just hang tight, we'll get you out of this. Everyone in school is going to know what's going on."

I hoped she was right.

Two hours later, there was a knock on the door and I went to answer it. To what I guess should not have been my surprise but actually was, there stood Anna and her father.

"Hi, Leon," she said.

"Hi, Anna," I said. "Hi, Warren." I reached out and shook her father's hand. "You guys wanna come inside?"

"Sure," he said. They stepped inside, and my dad, who had been in the kitchen with my mother, saw them coming.

Please, God, I thought, *don't let them be working on a food disaster.* I scanned the kitchen but didn't see anything more unusual than a box of noodles and a jar of spaghetti sauce.

"Hello there," he said, waving. "I'm Nick Harris."

"Warren Brandenburg," said Anna's dad, waving back. "And this is Anna."

Our dads shook hands, and I began to silently pray to whoever was listening that my father didn't act like a complete dork in front of Anna and her dad.

We all walked into the kitchen and sat down. My mother waved and introduced herself but stayed at the stove.

"So, Leon," said Anna's father, "I hear they're cracking down on you, huh?"

"You might say that," I said. "I should have shown up with rocks in my pockets."

"So you know about the project?" Dad asked.

"Of course. Anna's been working on it with him," said Mr. Brandenburg.

"Oh!" said my dad, as if he'd just discovered the Unified Theory of Everything. "You must be the one he borrowed the art books from."

"Right."

Dad sort of fixed me with a goofy grin, and I knew right away that the grin meant "You didn't tell me your friend was a girl!" I wanted to crawl into the nearest cave, but I didn't know of any caves in town, unless you counted the drainage ditch.

"Anyway," her dad continued, "I've had some run-ins with Mrs. Smollet before, and this is just the sort of thing I expect out of her. I wouldn't be surprised if she was looking for some way to suspend Anna, too. She's tried before."

"Really?" my dad asked.

"Yeah," Warren said. "We get calls from her now and then about some dumb thing or another. She usually warns that someone could sue. I thought if you and I, as parents, went in tomorrow, we could straighten this whole thing out and maybe get Leon off the hook before things get any worse."

"I was certainly planning on going in," said my father. "I think that this is clearly just the woman pushing her own agenda."

"I can guarantee it," said Mr. Brandenburg.

"Either that or she's just waiting for a good reason to sue them and get rich," I said.

"Probably both," said Mr. Brandenburg. "Or it might be a religious thing. This school has always been known to sort of skirt the boundary between church and state. Last year Anna's math teacher was always telling kids that they should buy some 'extreme teens' version of the New Testament."

"And no one would stop him," she said. "And the school team is named the Monks, after all. That's religious, too."

"And just plain stupid," I said.

"Well," said Anna's dad, "the story I've always heard was that it was supposed to be like Thelonious Monk, the piano player, but people thought it would be inappropriate to name the team after a jazz musician."

"Especially a black jazz musician," Anna added.

Her dad chuckled. "Probably that, too. It was back in the fifties, after all. But for one reason or another, they just had the mascot be a guy in robes to cover up the origin of the name."

"That sounds like a suburban myth," my dad said.

"I don't believe it, either," said Anna's dad. "It's probably just a dumb name all around, and that's that. But that's

150

sort of what we're up against. Still, I think we can get this taken care of."

My father got up to make coffee, and Mr. Brandenburg followed him over to the counter so they could make basic "nice to meet you, what kind of work do you do" small talk. I couldn't bear to listen to it; Anna's dad was probably the coolest parent in all of Cornersville, and my dad was probably going to come off as a doofus. However, their conversation left Anna and me alone at the table.

"Well," she said, almost whispering, "I told everyone."

"What do you mean?" I asked.

"I called everyone I know and told them to call everyone they know. Half the school is going to know about this by morning," she said.

"Coach Wilkins said he was telling people in his class," I said.

"Yeah, I heard he was," said Anna. "Some kid said he was calling you a political prisoner!"

"That's Wilkins for you," I said. "It's just like him to get all excited about something like this."

"Hell," she said, "it might work out well if he can get the kids excited about it."

"But half of them don't even like me very much," I said. "You'll get the gifted pool and maybe some of the headbangers rallied, but that's maybe twenty, thirty people. Most kids have never even met Smollet."

"Maybe we'll get more," she said. "It doesn't matter whether they like you. Even if they hate you, they probably still want to fight with Dr. Brown over this."

"We'll see, I guess," I said.

Meanwhile, our dads were still talking, and now my mother was talking with them, too; they all seemed to be getting along pretty well. Dad was talking about sound reception and flammable properties, so I guessed he was talking about his new invention, not the accounting job, which was probably good, as long as he never let anyone catch on that he wasn't a very good inventor.

Anyway, I was grateful that they had to leave before dinner was ready, since it turned out that the pasta and sauce were just the first two ingredients in a recipe that mixed tomato sauce with a sauce made out of zucchini that had been put in the blender. It actually didn't taste bad at all, but it was hard for me to want to eat something for which the recipe came out of a book called *Add Some Zucchini to Your Life!*

That, I said at the table, was not the title of a cookbook. It was a bad pickup line.

The next day I walked to school a hardened criminal. The original plan was for Dad to drop me off, but he decided he ought to pop into the Boredom Factory first, just to let them know he had some things to do and was taking a personal day. He and Anna's dad would be going into the school together later that morning.

So I walked. It wasn't a long walk; if I took the screen off my bedroom window and leaned out far enough, I could actually see the school on a clear day, though this was not the sort of thing I liked to do. When I was in my room, I generally preferred to think I was a safer distance away.

I arrived early and found Dr. Brown already waiting outside by the drainage ditch to escort me onto campus, but once we got past the parking lot I saw that the whole flagpole was surrounded by students—way more than there normally were. Brian was there, and so was Dustin, and a whole bunch of kids I didn't even know. As soon as they saw me, a bunch of people started shouting in my direction.

"Take 'em out, Leon!" someone shouted.

"Free Leon Harris!" shouted another.

Dr. Brown looked more than just a little annoyed; as soon as he saw me, he whisked me away and started leading me toward the front door, but just before he pulled me inside, I was able turn around and flash them a peace sign. Everyone—get this—cheered, like I was some sort of hero or something. A second later, through the door, I could hear a whole bunch of kids outside singing that Pink Floyd song that goes, "We don't need no education, we don't need no thought control."

"You've got quite a following today, Mr. Harris," said Dr. Brown as he hustled me down the hall.

"I told you everyone in school would know about this," I said, trying my hardest not to laugh at him. "My father is coming in to talk to you later."

"The one who hates Thomas Edison?"

"Gee," I said, figuring he'd heard that from Dr. Guff. "Some doctor-patient confidentiality you have around here."

"Interviews with students serving punishments aren't typically covered by that," said Dr. Brown. "But your father is welcome to come in. We have nothing to hide, and I'll be happy to speak to him."

I thought about asking why, if he had nothing to hide, he kept covering up his bald head with the cheap toupee, but I didn't. Honestly, I think the very fact that he had a cheap rug at all indicated that he probably wasn't principal material. When you're dealing with a bunch of middle school kids, appearance is everything. A nicer rug would have been worth the investment.

He led me straight to the in-school suspension room and shut the door, which annoyed me a bit, because school was still a few minutes from officially starting. Two minutes later, I heard a group of students in the hall chanting, "We are normal! We are normal!" I guessed Dustin had started that one.

I might have been an alleged smut peddler, but I felt invincible. Back in third grade, James Cole and I had somehow gotten the idea that no one ever died while people were clapping for them. We even got this idea that we could get some other people involved and arrange it so we were clapping for each other all the time when we got older, and hence, we'd never die. Of course, that was all nonsense. Plenty of people have been shot and killed while people were clapping for them. Still, the fact that people had cheered for me still made me feel somehow untouchable.

I had never considered myself particularly well liked at school. I didn't play sports. I didn't make out with anyone in the halls. Hell, the fact that I knew my heavy metal and knew enough not to go snitching on kids who were acting up were just about the only things that kept me from being a regular target for beat-downs. I knew that news about my being suspended would travel fast, but I never imagined that anyone would chant anything in the halls.

Suddenly, I had become popular.

And from what I had seen of the kids outside, it wasn't just the nerds and seminerds who liked me; even the dumbass kids who spent most of their classes chasing each other around and calling people fags were shouting and chanting. I guess no one could resist the idea of a movie with nudity in it.

I wasn't sure how I felt about being popular among those guys; I didn't really think I *wanted* them to like me. But that was what avant-garde art was all about. It was supposed to wake people up, make them look at things differently and stop acting like idiots, even if it was just for about five seconds. This may have been the first time in history, however, that it had actually worked.

After about twenty minutes, the door opened and Mr. Streich walked in.

"Hi, Leon," he said cheerfully. He raised a fist, like he was saying "right on." Normally I would have thought it was sort of patronizing, but the way Mr. Streich was grinning, I could see that he was on my side, not just teasing me. My dad had been right about him.

"What's up?" I asked. "Did they send you in here to interview me?"

"No," he said. "I just wanted to talk about your movie a bit. Your dad called me last night and told me that he'll be coming in to talk to Dr. Brown later, and I'm going to be there with him. I think your movie was really very creative, even if it was a little inappropriate."

"It wasn't inappropriate at all!" I said, for about the millionth time.

"Well, that's a matter of opinion," he said. "I don't really see the harm in it, but a lot of parents would. People get really touchy about that kind of thing, you know. But anyway, I'm giving you an A on it, even if you never finish it and they don't show it to a single kid."

"That's good," I said. "I was wondering about that." I had resigned myself to getting an F on the project, honestly, and even felt like it would be another badge of honor, but one less bad grade to worry about was nothing to whine over.

Just then, I heard someone outside the office shouting, "Free Leon!"

"Hear that?" He grinned. "You're a celebrity now."

"I noticed," I said. "I'm not sure what to think of it."

"Well, just don't let it go to your head," he warned. "Half of these kids'll forget all about it next week."

"Yeah, I know," I said. "But if they spend one day acting less like idiots, my work here is done."

He smiled again and said, "That's one way to look at it."

"This is all just Mrs. Smollet's fault," I said. "Her and Joe Griffin."

"Well," he said, "I don't agree with Mrs. Smollet all the time, either, but her opinions are valid, too, and it's important to remember that. Of course, that doesn't mean we have to let her run the world."

"I'll say," I said.

He patted my shoulder.

"It's gonna be quite a scene after school, I think," he said. "Coach Wilkins has been telling all the kids in his class that you're a political prisoner and that they should all show up to support you after school. But you didn't hear it from me." And he walked out of the room.

A few minutes later, I started to hear the sound of his voice, and the sound of my father's voice, and the sound of Mr. Brandenburg's voice, all talking to Dr. Brown, but I couldn't make out exactly what they were saying. Then I heard the sound of Mrs. Smollet talking, sounding all defensive.

Then they all stopped for a minute, and I saw a blue light under the door, which I guess meant that there was a TV showing the movie. I could just barely hear the narration being read out loud by Dr. Brown. After a few minutes, Mrs. Smollet spoke again. Then everyone spoke all at once, and then, in the middle of it, some kid in the hall shouted, "Free Leon Harris!" loudly enough that everyone could hear it in the office. I would have just about killed to be able to tell what was going on in that room. I moved up to the door and pressed my ear against it, but I still couldn't make out more than a word or two. Mrs. Smollet said "moral fiber" once, but she was the only one shouting loudly enough that I could hear anything she said. Everyone else was being a bit calmer.

It was only at this point that I realized that if I put my ear down on the floor, by the crack under the door, I could probably hear a lot better—some gifted kid I turned out to be. Hoping that no one would swing the door open and bash my head in, I got down on my knees to listen.

"Oh, heck," said my father's voice. "I probably go to church more often than you do."

"This is all like some sort of conspiracy," said Mrs. Smollet. "The two of you are raising a couple of little heathens, and I'm the one being persecuted! And just for trying to be religious!"

This was probably the first time I'd actually heard Mrs. Smollet claim to be religious herself—normally she just talked about being really moral. I guess she thought they were automatically the same thing.

"Now, let's calm down for a moment," said Dr. Brown, trying to play the peacekeeper. "No one's running any conspiracies here. I think we all need to take a deep breath. I'm not calling anyone's parenting skills into question."

"I am," said Mrs. Smollet.

If I hadn't known better than to do so, I would have charged in there and slugged her myself. Sure, I may complain about my dad—it's natural to complain when your parents are a few chicken tenders short of a sampler platter. But there was only one person who was going to call my dad a bad parent and get away with it—me.

"Muriel, please!" said Dr. Brown. I hadn't known that her first name was Muriel. I didn't know *anyone* was still called Muriel. "This project wasn't even a part of your class. Now, if you'll excuse us, the conference is between Mr. Harris, Mr. Brandenburg, and myself."

"And the devil makes four," she huffed. And I heard her get up and walk out, slamming the door behind her. I had to give her credit—that was a pretty good closing line.

No one said anything for a second or so. Then there was some muttering, so low that I couldn't even make it out with my ear practically in the room, and a couple of nervous chuckles. Then I heard everyone get up, and some doors open and shut, and I decided to get back in my seat before someone opened the door and took my head off.

Where the hell did Smollet get off? First, from what I gathered of the talk, she'd been telling my dad he didn't go to church enough; then she turned right around and said she was being persecuted for *her* religious beliefs? My dad probably *did* go to church more than she did. It would explain a lot if Mrs. Smollet was really a devil worshipper in disguise, and when we'd been pretending to be Satanists, she'd just been irritated that we weren't taking her dark lord seriously enough. At least Dr. Brown had had the good sense to kick her out of the room before I charged through the door and threw her out myself. Why had she taken a job as the gifted-pool director when all she wanted to do was play morality police?

I sat for a while, trying to get my mind off how pissed I was by scribbling down a list of what I still had to do to finish the movie in the notebook I had in my backpack. The list really just amounted to filming the kiss scene and explosion, recording the narration and music, and editing it all together.

The day went by a little bit faster than the day before had, partly because about every fifteen minutes I would hear some other kid walk up and shout, "Free Leon!" Waiting for that gave me something to do besides just eating my lunch.

It was early in the afternoon when the door opened and Mrs. Smollet walked in. She looked even more upset than she normally did, and was carrying a whole stack of papers.

"I hope you're happy, Leon," she said. "Do you have any idea how much trouble you've caused?"

"Well, I hear people shouting that you should let me go now and then," I said, not even bothering to keep myself from smiling.

"Did you put them up to that, Leon?" she asked, looking furious. "Are you behind all this?"

"Nope," I said. "If I'd asked them to, they never would have done it. Most of these kids probably hate me."

"Well, obviously they don't hate you that much."

It was right then that I realized what was happening. The jerks might have hated me, but they hated school even more. They weren't protesting for me, they were protesting against school. That was good enough for me.

"Maybe they don't, maybe they do," I said. "But it looks like they certainly hate you."

"This whole town is going to hell in a handbasket!" she muttered.

And she walked out, slamming the door behind her with a satisfying bang.

Ha.

I ended up in in-school suspension for the whole day after all, but Dr. Brown said he wouldn't have to escort me out. "I probably should," he said, "but your sentence is over, and it's probably better that I not go out there. It's you they're going to want."

"I'm sure there won't be a riot or anything," I said, though I wasn't really.

"I hope not," he said, shaking his head sternly, as if to warn me not to try to stir one up myself. "But there've been a lot of teachers saying that kids are shouting 'Free Leon'

161

and stuff like that in their classes. Coach Wilkins was trying to rally the teachers for you in the teachers' lounge. He made quite a scene, in fact."

"That sounds like him, all right," I said.

"For the record, I'd just like to say that I'm sorry all this happened. After talking to your dad and Mrs. Smollet today, it's fairly clear that she was overreacting. I always trust teachers' judgement when they want a student suspended, but I should have tried to calm her down first. There's a fine line between monitoring students' behavior and pushing your own agenda, and sometimes it gets a little blurry."

I didn't know quite how to respond to that. "Well, thanks," I said. "I can't say I was expecting to hear that."

"I'm not an ogre, Leon. I'm just a principal. And don't worry; as I said, I'm not letting this go on your permanent record."

When I stepped outside, probably thirty people were standing around the flagpole, where they were shouting out the words to that Pink Floyd song again. When they saw me, they stopped singing and cheered and clapped. Once again, I felt like I was invincible. As far as I know, I was. No one shot at me, so there was no way to tell for sure.

Coach Hunter, from gym, was standing in the background, watching with his arms folded and looking like he'd rather be shopping for women's shoes. I guessed that they'd sent him out there in case things got out of hand. In a way, this made him my bodyguard.

More people were chanting. I noticed Coach Wilkins was standing there, shouting, "Give art a chance!" and trying to get a chant going, though no one seemed to be going along with it. Still, I appreciated the gesture, and he looked like he was having all the fun in the world, shouting and carrying on and making a general fool of himself, trying to relive his wild, radical youth, I suppose.

I didn't have long to figure out who was there and who was doing what, though, because I was getting mobbed by kids who wanted to pat me on the back. I raised my arms and flashed peace signs with both hands. They cheered some more.

"When can we see the movie?" someone shouted.

"Soon!" I shouted out. "Victory party at Fat Johnny's tonight after the game!"

Technically, since I'd had to serve out the full day, it wasn't exactly a victory, but I had come out with my dignity intact, and the school sort of had its tail between its legs. That was enough of a victory for me.

All the kids from the gifted pool were there, along with a bunch of kids I just barely recognized, and a few more who I knew for a fact hated my guts. I guess when you're all going up against the school, no kids are enemies.

Meanwhile, Joe Griffin was standing off to the side, looking pretty pissed. I thought maybe I should go talk to him, but that wouldn't have been very nice. Like Mr. Streich said, his opinions were valid, too, and going over to rub his nose in the fact that his opinions didn't rule the world would have been ungraceful, like giving a guy an extra punch in a boxing match when he was already knocked out.

The whole thing didn't last very long, because half of the kids had to get on their buses before they were left behind. I guess you can't really get a good riot going when most of the rioters have to catch a bus. Within ten minutes I was walking home alone, but I felt like a king.

Dad was waiting on the front porch.

"You should have seen it, Dad!" I said. "People were chanting and screaming and everything."

Dad grinned. "It seems like you were a pretty popular guy today," he said.

"It's weird," I said. "I never saw that coming."

"You wanna know how the conversation went at the school?" he asked.

"More than anything," I admitted. "I heard the last minute or so under the door, but I didn't hear most of the beginning."

"Well, Max Streich met me in front of the office, and we went in to talk to the principal. We were mostly talking about how we thought the school was going too far. Then Anna's father showed up and said the same thing. Then that one lady, Mrs. Smollet, came in. She's quite a piece of work, isn't she?"

"That's one way to put it."

"She told us that if she had her way, you would be expelled altogether, or at least removed from the gifted program. Then she went into this rant about how your mother and I must be horrible parents."

"She actually said that?" I asked. "I just heard her sort of hint it."

"I almost didn't believe it, but she said that, all right. Then she told Anna's father he was extremely lucky that his daughter wasn't in just as much trouble. And something about how expecting a moral, Christian woman like her to work among miscreants like you made it a hostile work environment, which she could sue over."

"Sounds like her, all right."

"Right about then, I think Dr. Brown was starting to see that she was a little out of hand."

"Really?"

"Yes. He suggested we all watch the movie, and we did."

"Yeah, I noticed you were all watching it. Too bad it wasn't done or anything."

He nodded. "It was good, Leon. I don't know if it will change the world or anything, but it was very creative. I said afterward that I didn't really see what she was so upset about, and Anna's father said that it had a lot of artistic merit. Then she really hit the roof and basically blamed us for all the problems of youth and the lack of moral fiber in the community."

"She really loves to talk about moral fiber," I said.

"It's an old trick," said Dad. "People call their way of living moral, so it looks like everyone who disagrees with them is some kind of criminal. But I told her that she shouldn't worry, because your mother kept you off the bus so you couldn't have oral sex on it."

I laughed. "Seriously?"

"I sure did. Your mother and I sort of disagree on that. I think it's a bit silly. But it makes her feel better."

This was interesting news.

"What did Mrs. Smollet say to that? At some point I heard you say we go to church more than she does."

"I said that, and I meant it," he said. "I'm not very religious, really. You know that. But I certainly know a bit about the basics of theology, and I know that there are certain people who probably aren't really religious at all, they just use religion to back up their own agenda, and they usually don't know a thing about theology. But I said it, and she started playing the victim, saying that we had come in to scream at her and all that, even though we hadn't raised our voices. After she left, Dr. Brown said that he'd look into the whole thing right away, and herded us out. I think he was a bit embarrassed by the way Mrs. Smollet was acting."

"I think so, too," I said. "He sort of even apologized."

"Really? That's a step in the right direction."

"I would have fired her if I were him," I said.

"I suppose you could make a case for that," said my dad. "But learning to deal with people like her is just a part of life. If you can learn that, you'll get a lot more use out of it than most of the stuff they teach you in class."

We sat silently for a few seconds. "Leon," he said finally, "I just want you to know that I'm proud of you. I really am. I don't think anyone can make a living making avant-garde films, but you had an idea and you went for it. That's worth a lot in this world."

"Yeah," I said. "But I think I want to go to film school instead of accounting school."

He looked at me with a raised eyebrow. "You were planning on going to accounting school?"

"Well, no," I said. "But I sort of assumed that you wanted me to do something like that."

He sort of chuckled. "Leon," he said, "you haven't scored higher than a C-plus in math the whole time you've been in middle school. I sort of assumed you weren't planning on a career in accounting."

He patted my knee and walked inside.

I didn't know what to say. Or how to feel.

Thinking back, I realized that he had never actually said I should be an accountant—had never said anything of the sort, in fact. But in the back of my mind, I'd always sort of thought that he wanted me to do something boring. It felt good to have that weight off my back, but I didn't know if I wanted him to be proud of me any more than I wanted those jerks from school to think I was a hero. Any normal dad probably would have grounded me.

As we have seen, though, my dad was simply not normal.

14

I walked into Fat Johnny's feeling like a hero that night, but I wanted to talk to my friends more than I wanted to play the part. I snuck in quietly and joined Edie, Brian, and Anna at a table before anyone could see me.

"Did you hear the news?" asked Anna.

"Which news?" I asked.

"Smollet's giving up the gifted-pool job!"

My eyes got so wide it's a wonder they didn't fall right out into Anna's Coke.

"Are you serious?"

She grinned. "Dr. Brown called and told my dad this afternoon. She's going to just focus on whatever it is she does at the high school instead."

"Oh my God," I said. "Do you know what this means? We actually won. We beat the school system!"

"Cheers!" shouted Brian. And he waved his lighter above his head.

A lot people noticed the flame in the air and then noticed that I was there, and suddenly I had ten or fifteen people coming up to pat me on the back and congratulate me on being free. I knew they'd probably all go back to hating me pretty soon, so I figured I should just enjoy it while I could.

No fewer than twenty people asked when they could see the movie over the course of the night. And these were eighth graders, not the sixth and seventh graders who were supposed to see it—if it hadn't been banned, they probably never would have even heard of it. Clearly, the school hadn't been able to do anything to keep people from wanting to see the movie. Coach Wilkins was right about that whole Judy Blume business.

"You know," said Brian, after people had gone back to talking about the football game and cheating at Skee-Ball, "they say that there's nothing that'll make a song a hit faster than banning it."

"I think you're right," I said. "Half the kids in school are probably dying to see what all the fuss was about."

"More than that," said Anna. "Probably all of them. So we have to finish up."

"Mr. Streich'll still let us use the editing gear for it, won't he?" I asked.

"He won't have to," said Brian. "He already loaned it to me. As soon as we film the kiss scene and you get the explosion and the narration and stuff, I can edit it all together. And I can put it on the computer and make all the hard copies we need."

"And now that it's not a school project, I can have the explosion!" I said.

Suddenly there was a tap on my shoulder, and I turned to see Joe Griffin.

"They, uh . . . they shouldn't have suspended you," he said sheepishly.

"What?" I asked. I genuinely would never have predicted that—so much for my psychic powers. "You were the one who told Dr. Brown I was encouraging people to whack off."

"Yeah, but . . . I didn't think he'd suspend you, I just thought he wouldn't show the younger kids the movie. Sorry about that."

And, before I could say anything else, he sort of slinked away. Brian, Edie, Anna, and I stared at each other.

"What the hell was that?" asked Brian

"Maybe his dad told him he could get sued for something," said Edie.

"I don't care, that was nice of him," I said. "Man, even my worst enemies are on my side now."

It was beginning to look like being banned was the best thing that had ever happened to the movie—or to me. I was feeling like the king of all suburbia, and the movie was poised to be not just a film to educate the sixth and seventh graders, but also the biggest film ever to hit Cornersville Trace. All we needed was the explosion, the kissing scene, the music, and the narration.

I wasn't afraid of anything anymore. If I wasn't doing it as an official school project, there was nothing to stop me from doing an explosion.

Brian showed up early the next day with a whole box of wires and recording gear.

170

"I think the way to do it," he said, "will be to run the mikes through your stereo. That way we can blast the instruments through the wall of sound, and then you can stand in the hall and record the narration, so you won't be drowned out."

"Wouldn't it be easier to just record it all without any amps? I could just stand closer to the recording mike or something."

"That might be easier," he said, "but it wouldn't be as cool."

He had me there. He busied himself adding resistors and I don't know what-all to the speakers and wires, getting everything together and saying that they would help it from blowing a fuse. Midway through, he stumbled upon a book of Dad's not-quite-self-lighting matches, and I explained what they were supposed to be.

"Dude," he said, "if he can get these things to work, I'll buy them by the pound." Apparently, being able to start a fire with the snap of one's fingers was every pyromaniac's dream. He didn't know exactly how Dad could go about getting them to work properly, though. He was better with mechanics than he was with chemistry.

Shortly thereafter, Dustin came over with a keyboard, Anna brought her cello, and Jenny Kurosawa's dad dropped her off with her clarinet.

Once everybody was there, Brian went about the process of getting everything rigged up, with microphones all around to catch everything. Dustin, Jenny, and Anna jammed a bit, playing a bluesy sort of riff that sounded a little more coherent than I'd expected. They played together

171

pretty well, and it was pretty rocking, considering that the band was just a piano, a cello, and a clarinet.

"Sounds like early Led Zeppelin," I said. "Only with different instruments."

"Classic rock, man!" said Dustin, jamming away and hitting the keys with his elbow for show. Brian, meanwhile, was surrounded by so many cords that it was a wonder he wasn't choking to death. All the instruments were hooked to pickups that ran into the stereo, and the sound would be blared out on my half wall full of speakers. Brian had added some resistors or something that he said would keep the circuit from blowing again, but he said that the whole thing would probably be incredibly loud anyway. That was fine with me. I rigged up the camera on the dresser to film the whole recording, in case I ever wanted to put together a making of *La Dolce Pubert* movie or something like that.

I went out in the hall with a separate microphone to record the narration, since it was going to be way too loud in the room to read anything.

"Okay," I shouted. "I'm going to start reading. You guys start playing after the first line."

"Got it!" Dustin shouted back.

"All the mikes are hooked to the stereo," shouted Brian, "and we're recording . . . now!"

I took a deep breath and read out, "We were weirdos once, and young," then heard what was absolutely the loudest piano chord I'd ever heard coming through the speakers, so loud that I'm pretty sure the walls rattled a bit, and then everything went quiet.

At first I thought maybe the circuit had blown again, but then Brian shouted, "Leon! Hurry!"

I ran into the room and saw that the entire book of matches had caught fire—apparently, the problem with them was that a snap wasn't loud enough to get them going.

"Put it out!" I shouted. Brian opened up the can of Coke that had been sitting on my desk and poured it all over the matches, which would probably wreck half of the things on my desk.

It was just then that I remembered that the book on my table was far from being the bulk of the flammable material in the house.

"Oh, no!" I shouted. "The garage!"

We all ran down the stairs to the garage, where, sure enough, Dad was busily trying to put out a whole bunch of little fires with the fire extinguisher. He looked absolutely thrilled.

"They work!" he shouted, between fire extinguisher blasts. "You got them working!" It was just like him to be absolutely delighted that the garage was on fire.

"Dad!" I shouted. "The chemicals!"

One of the lab coats was on fire, and the fire was slowly creeping its way toward a beaker full of the blue gunk that he'd been using for the tips of the matches. He turned to look at the coat, but it was too late—the whole beakerful of chemicals caught fire at once, in a huge burst of flames that went most of the way up to the ceiling and caught the table below it on fire.

"Damn!" he shouted, pointing the fire extinguisher at

what was left of the beaker. It was hotter than hell in there, and was starting to look a bit like hell is supposed to look, too. Mrs. Smollet's prediction that the town was going there in a handbasket might not have been as far off as I'd thought!

A minute later, it was all over. The fire was out, and the whole garage was covered in white gunk from the extinguisher. No one had died, and the only real casualties were a lab coat, the table, and a bunch of lab equipment. It was a miracle that the explosion hadn't hurt anyone.

It was only then that I realized that Dustin, ever the resourceful fellow, had brought the camera down from the bedroom and, at great risk to his own life and limb, had gotten the whole thing on tape. When we played it back, it looked like one hell of an explosion—it was perfect!

After we all helped clean the garage (before my mother, who, thankfully, was at the mall, could find out), we went back to my room, where we recorded the whole thing straight, without using the wall of sound at all, like I'd suggested in the first place. It sounded fine and was an awful lot easier, even if it wasn't quite as cool.

That night, my mother grounded me for a week for burning the garage down after she noticed all the char marks on the walls, which made no sense to me at all. Dad had been fine with me experimenting with the speakers before, even after they blew a fuse, and it was his gear, not mine, that had caught fire. It had only been my fault in a tiny, tiny way.

Still, I never thought I would be the one in the family who burned the garage down. Dad seemed to have a lock on that one.

The next day was to be the day we recorded the kissing scene, but Brian called me up in the morning.

"I have some bad news."

"Oh yeah?" I asked.

"Edie has decided that she's against kissing."

"What the hell? You guys kiss all the time!"

"Yeah, but now she thinks that communists shouldn't kiss. I'm not really clear on why."

"But that'll never last, will it? She'll be kissing you again by Tuesday for sure."

"Probably," he said. "But I can't talk her into doing the scene today."

My mind started racing. I needed that scene done, and fast. If I waited, interest in the movie might die down by the time we got it finished.

"Well," I said, "if I get another couple to do it, will you still be able to edit it this afternoon?"

"Sure."

"I'll bring it by when it's ready, then."

I hung up without saying good-bye and stared at the wall. My hand was shaking. But it was then or never. I knew what I had to do.

I picked up the phone and dialed Anna's number.

The rest of the day was like a total blur. Talking to Anna on the phone, hearing her say she'd stand in. Waiting for her to come over. Setting up the camera so that you could see both of us standing together. And kissing her. Long and hard and good. On camera.

I had never kissed anyone quite that way before and

didn't have anything to measure it against. But it sure seemed like a good kiss to me. I would have gone for second, third, and fourth takes, but I was afraid she'd call me on it, so I had to be as businesslike as possible. I didn't let her know that when I hit Record I was so nervous I could hardly stand up. I was afraid my knees, which were knocking like crazy, would bump into hers, and maybe even knock her over. But I got through it. And, in complete defiance of being grounded (we were operating outside the law to begin with, right?), I got on my bike to take the footage over to Brian's house.

She rode her bike next to me, and then we both watched Brian as he put it all on his computer, then edited all the scenes into the right order and added the music and narration. The kiss looked pretty good to me on the screen, and following it with an explosion, which was almost immediately covered in white gunk from the fire extinguisher, was pretty obvious sexual symbolism, but it worked for me. The explosion was accompanied by one loud, long piano chord that faded out while the white gunk doused the flames, and it smoldered right along with the fire, which was really cool, especially considering that we hadn't quite planned it that way.

The movie was finished.

A week later, I'm pretty sure that every kid in school, from sixth through eighth grade, had seen La Dolce Pubert. Some of them got a copy that Brian posted on the Internet; some saw the copies that we made and passed around. Within a couple of weeks, there wasn't a kid left who wanted to see it but hadn't. This probably made it much more popular than your average short avant-garde film, because almost nobody sees most of them.

As I might have expected, most of them hated it and went right back to hating me, on account of its being so weird. Lots of the younger kids thought it was great, mostly because it showed some naked paintings and used the word "whacking" several times. But I think a few of them also really felt relieved about hearing that they were normal, and nobody picked on me over that, which was sort of a relief.

It may not have changed the way people think about puberty or torn down any laws of society, but all things considered, the movie did what I hoped it would in the first place, and it helped get Mrs. Smollet out of the gifted pool at the same time. We'd still have to put up with her in high school, but we would be able to enjoy a good eight months of school without her.

Not half bad for a first try.

15

October is a big month in the weirdo calendar. Not that there's really such thing as a weirdo calendar, as far as I know, though they do seem to be putting out a lot of nutty calendars these days. It's just an expression. Anyway, if there was a weirdo calendar, they'd probably have to have October be three or four extra pages, just to make room. The month of Halloween is a big one. The weather gets colder, the leaves change colors, and the Halloween decorations start coming up, and all of a sudden people are celebrating weird stuff instead of calling it "gay."

Starting right about October 1, we kicked things into high gear. Dustin wrote up lyrics for a bunch of songs based on Christmas carols that were changed around to be about ghosts and witches and other Halloween stuff. Stuff like "People Roasting on an Open Fire," "Zombie the Snowman," and my personal favorite, to the tune of "Away in a Manger":

Away in a graveyard, no crypt for a bed,
The ghosts and the zombies
All want to be fed.
They took all the teachers
And sucked out their brains,
But in no time at all
They were hungry again!

We printed up a few dozen copies of the lyrics and scattered them in various places around the school where people would be sure to find them. Dustin and I both got called into the office and questioned about them, since they had a pretty good idea that we were behind it, but they couldn't prove anything, so we got off.

Closer to the end of the month, several of the other films made in the class were shown to the sixth and seventh graders. Anna's was a huge hit, especially because a couple of teachers objected to the subject matter. Dustin's went over well, because he had an awful lot of blood and gore in it. He said that he'd used about ten bottles of ketchup, which is enough to provide blood for quite a few action figures, which he used as the crash victims. I was a little annoyed that they let something so violent be shown, but not something that dealt with sex. But it didn't really matter; everyone had already seen *La Dolce Pubert* anyway. I got the feeling that this would be the only time they assigned kids the task of making health and safety films to show to younger kids.

In light of the fact that the school would have no power over us after the end of the year, we'd made plans to steal some of the actual health, safety, and science films from the back room of the school and replace them with copies of *La Dolce Pubert*. By the time anyone found out about it, we'd all be safely in ninth grade, and, since so many kids had copies, they'd never be able to prove that we were behind the whole thing, anyway.

Mr. Streich took over the gifted pool, and the whole thing got a lot better. We actually started having discussions and doing real projects instead of just crossword puzzles and brain teasers, though we still had to do the thing where we researched someone from the past. I picked Thomas Edison and found out that my dad was right—the guy really was sort of a jerk. He was selfish, greedy, and sneaky, and he took credit for inventing things when his staff had done all the work. He once even electrocuted a full-grown elephant just to prove a point, which was a hell of a mean thing to do. I still want to change my middle name the day I turn eighteen, though.

Anna and I still aren't exactly dating, but we kissed twice in the month after the scene was shot, once during a truth or dare game at Brian's house and once when we acted out a scene from a Shakespeare play in English class, which was cool because no one actually expected us to do it; we were just supposed to fake it. I hoped we could do it more often, though I wasn't brave enough to ask.

My dad gave up on the idea of the self-lighting matches, on the grounds that they were simply too dangerous (my mother insisted), and decided to start working on a machine that would automatically get the seeds out of watermelons. So far he hadn't done much besides make a huge mess, but at least this kind of mess isn't likely to break any-thing other than a few vacuum cleaner engines. Personally, I hope he finishes it soon. Since he's been working on it, we've had to eat an alarming number of watermelons, which has led my mother to dig deep into books like *Watermelons for Health* and *How Famous Chefs Use Watermelon*. I have to wonder exactly what these chefs were famous *for*.

Speaking of food disasters, my parents started making plans to go to some convention for food disaster hobbyists that was going to be in Omaha around Christmas. I was sur-prised that such a convention existed; I was sort of under the impression that my parents were the only such hobby-ists who hadn't died of food poisoning by now.

"They're expecting a hotel full of people," said my mother. "And we're going to get to try some of the worst stuff ever made."

"One whole day is devoted to making things out of cookbooks from the Depression," said my father, showing me the brochure, which was absolutely hideous. "Back then, they encouraged people to use every single part of the cow." There was a picture in the brochure of something that looked about like snot and was labeled "Creamed Brains on Toast," which practically made me want to become a vege-tarian. Elsewhere in the brochure, it mentioned that the bar would be serving drinks that came out of a recipe book from the seventies for cocktails that mixed liquor with Tang.

I wasn't going, of course, which meant that I would have the house to myself on Halloween—except for my mother's sister, Rachel, who'd be coming over to keep an eye on me and make sure I didn't set the garage on fire again. But Aunt

181

Rachel was pretty laid back, and I knew she wouldn't mind me throwing a Halloween party. Dustin had the idea of asking everyone to dress up as a character out of an old book, and he'd be able to tell us all the characters we were sleeping with. I decided to dress up as Dr. Jekyll; I was pretty sure that he really got around. And given that my parents wouldn't be home and Aunt Rachel would probably just be up in their bedroom watching TV, I figured I could actually manage to do some getting around myself. A game of truth or dare certainly didn't seem out of the question.

On Halloween night, in the early evening, about an hour before the party was supposed to start, I was in the kitchen trying to get my top hat to look just bent enough when I heard the doorbell ring. It was Anna, dressed up like Captain Hook (I could just imagine what Dustin would say he was doing with Smee) and holding some paper.

"I have a script," she said.

"For what?" I asked.

"The next avant-garde movie."

I invited her in and she sat down at the table while I brewed a pot of coffee, something I was getting pretty good at doing by then. I had planned on making another movie at some point but hadn't really had time to think about what I wanted to do. I wasn't just going to rest on my laurels, though.

When I sat down, she handed me the script, which was labeled *The Rooster in the Skating Rink: A Musical (based on a true story)*.

It was a much longer script than *La Dolce Pubert*, and

actually seemed to have a plot of some sort. There were characters listed on the front page, including:

> Professor Earl Gray: an inspector from Scotland Yard with a wooden leg and a penchant for chamomile tea and kick-boxing
>
> The Divine Miss Madeline Brooch: a time-traveling cabaret singer from 1890s Paris
>
> Arthur: a talking plant who speaks French and would also speak sign language if he had any hands

"It looks like this actually has a plot," I said, scanning it.

"It sort of does," she said, "though it doesn't make a whole lot of sense, so it's still avant-garde. Or at least surreal. Anyway, I'm going to play the Divine Miss Madeline Brooch, and you can be Professor Earl Gray. Check it out. I thought maybe we could rehearse a scene or two before everyone else gets here."

As the coffee machine began making noise, indicating that the coffee would be ready in a few minutes, I flipped through the script, and a smile spread across my face.

The Divine Miss Madeline Brooch and Professor Earl Gray were clearly the stars of the show.

And they had kissing scenes on every page.

ABOUT THE AUTHOR

Adam Selzer grew up in the suburbs of Des Moines and now lives in downtown Chicago, where he can write in a different coffee shop every day without even leaving his neighborhood. In addition to his work as a tour guide and assistant ghost-buster (really), he moonlights as a rock star. *How to Get Suspended and Influence People* is his first novel. Check him out on the Web at www.adamselzer.com.

DATE DUE

GAYLORD   PRINTED IN U.S.A.